BLUE SKIES

AND

TAIL WINDS

GERRY COLE

STRATTON
—**PRESS**—
Publishing Life

BLUE SKIES AND TAIL WINDS
Copyright © 2021 **GERRY COLE**

Stratton Press Publishing
831 N Tatnall Street Suite M #188,
Wilmington, DE 19801
www.stratton-press.com
1-888-323-7009

ISBN (Paperback): 978-1-64895-526-6
ISBN (Hardback): 978-1-64895-528-0
ISBN (Ebook): 978-1-64895-527-3

Printed in the United States of America

To my family:

Jeremy, Matt, Leah, and Shayna.
You light up my life, and I love you all more than you know!

CHAPTER
ONE

I cannot believe I am sitting here with my son, Matt. As I look around me, I see people in the room who are missing limbs. One has both legs gone; another has an amputated arm. My son is also an amputee. That is not an adjective I like using to describe him, but it is the reality of what has happened to him. I realize today, six years after the accident almost took his life, that life goes on, and what we make of our lives is up to us. Matt is my twenty-nine year old son, my first-born, one of my three most treasured possessions. He had his right arm amputated up to the elbow in November 2006. I thought I was prepared for the finality of this operation, but as he was wheeled to the operating room, optimistic as usual, I found myself falling apart once again and was grateful that my husband, Jeremy, was with me to help pick up the pieces.

Matt made the decision to have his arm amputated in early 2006. He talked about it with his dad and me, and we tried to weigh all the pros and cons. We made lists and then we talked about it some more. Matt's philosophy was very realistic. He said his arm and hand was useless, and none of the doctors we consulted gave us any hope that they could repair all the damaged tissue in Matt's forearm. We had taken Matt to Jewish Hand Hospital in Louisville, Kentucky, and were told Matt was a good candidate for a hand transplant. The caveat was the need for immunosuppressants for the rest of his life. We felt these drugs can be dangerous. Yes, they do a world of good if you really need them, but this surgery was elective. Matt agreed.

As the year wore on, Matt became more anxious. He wanted the operation and wanted to get on with life. He told us there was so much he wanted to do, but could not because his hands were nonfunctional, and even though he enjoyed his life, there was more he wanted to accomplish. We could not argue with him, so we gave him out support and went with him to the surgery center on a cold morning in mid-November. When we arrived, I signed all the necessary papers for Matt, and he was taken to the holding area where he would be prepared for surgery.

Jeremy and I were left in the waiting room, but we had decided the night before that we would not rehash the last five years because it was too painful and we had been through all this before. We were now in "moving on" mode.

When we were called back to the holding area, we were greeted by a very hopeful Matt, who was joking with the nurses and anxiously awaiting his turn at surgery. We met the anesthesiologist who had given Matt a nerve block. We were surprised to learn that Matt would be given Versed to relax him and the nerve block, which would numb his arm. Theoretically, if he did not relax or fall asleep, his arm would be amputated while he was awake. I was only mildly shaken up because I trusted the doctor and knew they would take good care of my son.

While Matt was in surgery, Jeremy and I drove to the pharmacy to fill his prescriptions. The line was long, and it took a while to get his medications. When we returned to the surgery center, we were surprised to learn that Matt was out of the operating room, was doing well in recovery, and would be ready to go home as soon as he drank a glass of soda and ate a few crackers. I just could not believe it. Despite the severity of the operation, we would take Matt home in less than six hours. Once again, I felt the gnawing in my stomach that I had grown so accustomed to while Matt was in the hospital after his accident. I was frightened of the unknown and could not foresee that would happen once Matt was at home with me.

Matt was in good spirits when his dad and I walked into the recovery room. He was sitting up in a chair and was joking with all the nurses. The IV had been disconnected from his foot, his vital signs were normal, he was drinking 7 UP, and he was on the road to recovery.

He said, "Hi, Mom and Dad. It's a good day. Today is the beginning of the rest of my life."

Shame on me for being so distraught. Since Matt's accident six years ago, I have learned a lot from my son. I have learned about perseverance and how to keep going even though I might be too tired. Matt has taught me how to be more patient and to not crave things for the moment.

We arrived home in early afternoon, and Jeremy promptly left for the hospital to make rounds on his own patients. That left me at home with Matt. I am not a nurse, so I always imagine the worst-case scenario. I worried about his blood pressure dropping or the nerve block wearing off, causing excruciating pain, or him getting nauseous from the medication and I would not be able to control it. None of those things happened. Matt was tired, so I elevated his arm on two pillows, and he fell asleep with his dog at the foot of the bed.

A week later, we had an appointment with the surgeon. He took all the bandages off and was very pleased that Matt was healing so quickly. He told us to call the prosthetist immediately and start working on a prosthetic arm for Matt. He felt it would be better for Matt to have a prosthesis as quickly as possible so he could start practicing and become proficient at using the arm.

We had our first appointment on a cold, blustery morning in December, and we were introduced to Mark Ridgely, who would work with Matt and make the prosthesis for him. Unfortunately, Matt's stump had a lot of swelling and the skin was red and had what appeared to be a rash. We had been worried about his skin after the amputation. The skin had been burned and grafted and had been very delicate since the beginning. Mark could not begin to make the arm until the swelling and redness subsided.

We waited for about six weeks before Mark felt the skin was tough enough to support a very tight-fitting device. Finally, he took us to the room where he would "cast" the prosthesis. Matt was ecstatic and could not hide his elation. It was amazing to see how far Matt, and our family, had come since that fateful day in March 2001. We had survived a terrible ordeal, and we even landed on out feet. Some of us had more difficulty, but, nonetheless, we all passed with flying colors.

CHAPTER
TWO

March 16, 2001, started out like any early spring day in Southern California, but I was feeling particularly lazy and wished I could stay in bed. I went through my daily routine. I made a cup of cappuccino, fed the family labs, saw my youngest daughter off to school, and kissed my husband goodbye as he left for work.

I also received a phone call from Matt, who was living in Daytona Beach, Florida. He was taking classes at Embry Riddle Aeronautical University and working at Phil Air Flight Center as a flight instructor. He told me he would be taking a standardization flight in a multi-engine Seneca airplane in the afternoon. He would be accompanied by his boss, Phil Herron, who would administer the practical test. Passing this test would enable Matt to instruct in this aircraft. As usual, I wished Matt blue skies and tailwinds. We agreed to speak in the evening.

Jeremy and I had just sold our house in Tarzana, California, and were hoping to settle into something smaller since the kids were growing up and, one by one, were leaving the nest. My afternoon would be busy looking for houses to buy. I happened to be in a neighbourhood in Tarzana looking at a beautiful house only about two blocks from where we had lived for about twenty years when I saw a white car turn the corner and start honking the horn. As the car approached me, I saw it was my daughter, Leah. She was hysterical.

She screamed at me, "Mom, get in the car. There's been an accident. Matt's plane crashed, and they don't know if he's alive!"

I felt something close to my heart stomping on my toes. I am sure my real estate lady thought I had completely lost it, because I think I started to scream.

All I could get out was, "What happened?"

Leah did not have any details, and I could not move fast enough to get into the car. My feet were frozen to the pavement, and I thought I was going to be sick. My knees started to buckle, and I began to shake uncontrollably, but I still could not move.

I continued screaming, "What happened! My god, what happened?"

Somehow I made it into Leah's car and looked at her face. She was crying, and I am not sure how we made it home. By now, I, too, was crying, and I think I remember saying something like, "Please, God, anything but not my child. Don't take my child!"

When we arrived home, Maria, our housekeeper, met me in the driveway and helped me into the house. We went to Leah's room and listened to the message left on the answering machine.

It was one of the guys from flight school where Matt worked, and he said, "Uh, yes, Mrs. Cole, there has been an accident. Matt's plane went down. We don't know exactly where. We don't know if he's alive. Sorry." And he hung up the phone.

Leah, Maria, and I just stood in the middle of the room, not knowing what to do. I think one of us started to cry again, but I am not sure which. The phone call is one that no parent wants or should ever receive. I now had to find my son, so I started making phone calls. First, I called Phil-Air Flight School in Dayton Beach, Florida, where Matt worked as a flight instructor, and I spoke to a young man named Dan. He and Matt had flown together a number of times, and they were friends. He told me a multi-engine plane carrying Matt and two other flight instructors had gone down near Flagler, Florida, a few miles north of Daytona Beach. He said to try calling Flagler Hospital, where Matt might be.

On my first try, I was connected to the emergency room, and I hit pay dirt. I spoke with a woman who I assumed was the emergency room doctor, and she said, "Yeah, we have Matt Cole here."

When I asked about his status, she said," He's alive, but I don't know for how long."

Her harsh, insensitive words hit me like a bullet in the chest. I could not speak. I mumbled my concern and finally was able to tell her that I am Matt's mother. She told me that Matt had been badly burned, and she had put him on a respirator to assist his breathing as a precautionary measure. She said it was too early to tell if Matt had internal injuries, but a preliminary examination determined he had no broken bones and a CAT scan showed he did not have a head injury. Thankfully, my husband walked in, and I handed the phone to him. I just was unable to talk to this lady anymore. She told my husband also that Matt had been badly burned, and he was breathing with the help of a ventilator. She said she did not know about inhalation injury because it was too early to tell. She also told Jeremy that she was stabilizing Matt so he could be airlifted to Shands Hospital at the University of Florida in Gainesville.

Our next task was to find a way to get to Gainesville as soon as possible. We called a number of airlines and finally got a flight out at midnight on Delta Airlines. The truth be told, we really were unfamiliar with Gainesville. We thought it was in Georgia. Matt's girlfriend, Tricia, and numerous friends were calling us wanting to know what happened and how Matt was doing. We had no answer for anyone. We could only tell them he was in Shands Hospital in Gainesville, and Jeremy and I and our two daughters, Matt's sisters, would be on our way at midnight.

Our friends of many years, Sona and Mark Rosenberg, came over to lend support and help us get ready for our departure. Sona offered to feed our dogs for the weekend until the guy who always boarded them got back to town and could pick them up. Sona also helped me pack a suitcase because I could not remember what I would need to take with me, and she and Mark took us to a deli to eat. We Coles just sat there not knowing what to say. I think I cried through dinner and had to excuse myself to go to the ladies' room numerous times.

As we were leaving the restaurant, Jeremy's cell phone rang. It was a nurse named Kerry who was calling from the burn unit at Shands Hospital. We never found out how she tracked us down, and she will probably never know how much her phone call meant to us. She told us Matt had been flown in by helicopter and was admitted as a patient to the burn intensive care unit. He would be debrided. That means his skin would be scraped of as much burned materials as possible. He had already been placed in a drug-induced coma so he would feel no pain. Jeremy gave her our health insurance information and told her we were on our way to the airport. She told us Matt's vital signs were stable, but with burn patients, one never knew when they would take a turn for the worse.

LAX was congested, as usual, and we had to battle the traffic. We told Mark and Sona to drop us off at the terminal, but they did not like that idea. They parked the car and came to the gate with us. They saw us off with kisses and prayers for Matt and hopes for his recovery. At that moment, we did not know if our son would be alive when we arrived in Gainesville, and that was the longest flight of my life. The flight attendant kept replenishing my tissue supply and asking me if I needed anything.

When we deplaned in Atlanta, we had another wait at another gate before our short flight to Gainesville took off. A very petite girl with glasses and blonde curls came up to me and asked me if I was Matt's mom. She explained that she was Tricia's friend, Lisa, and she was coming to Florida to support Tricia. We sat together on the plane, and she explained that on her last visit to Daytona Beach, Matt had rented a plane, and he, Tricia, and Lisa flew to Merritt Island, off the coast of Florida, had dinner together, and had a delightful evening flight back to Daytona Beach. She told me how comfortable she'd felt with Matt as pilot-in-command.

Finally, we arrived at our destination. Jeremy, my daughters Leah and Shayna, and I could not get off the plane fast enough. There were too many passengers, and we had to wait our turn.

We were met at the airport by a couple of Matt's pilot friends from Daytona Beach and Tricia, his girlfriend. When we saw each other, Tricia and I hugged each other and cried a little together. She was very upset that she had not been given any information regarding Matt's status. She was told since she was not Matt's wife, no one from the burn unit would speak to her. I understood this protocol, but it was not the time to explain it to her.

It was a gorgeous sunny and warm day, but it was a bleak day for me. I felt numb, and I was not able to speak. The friends had spent the night on the floor outside the burn unit, and Tricia told us that a woman kept coming out to update them, and she assured them she would let them know if Matt died. I can imagine how frightened those kids got every time she showed her face. A few days later, I had the opportunity to meet her and found out she was the ward clerk. This was my first annoyance. Even if she had knowledge of a patient's death, it would not be up to her to inform the family. I had bigger fish to fry, so I let it go. Down the road, I felt much better about not opening my mouth.

When we arrived at the burn unit on the seventh floor, we were told we had to wait while someone was doing a procedure on Matt. We joined Matt's friends on the floor and waited for about an hour. Finally, a heavyset nurse named Alan came to get us and escorted us to the conference room, where we met Dr. Jason Rosenberg. We were told that Matt was stable, but was burned over 60 percent of his body from the waist up. His burns would require skin grafts and then releases, and physical therapy down the road. His recovery would be long and difficult. I think everything they were saying went in one ear and right out the other. I could not think straight, and I certainly could not focus. I was trying to be strong and not cry, but I was not succeeding. I was looking at everyone, but I did not really see them.

Dr. Rosenberg said that Matt was a strong, healthy young man with no risk factors, and he would probably survive if an infection of some sort did not attack his body. Those were not great odds, but they were better than nothing. Finally, Jeremy, Leah, Shayna, Tricia, and I were escorted to a closet area, where we put on yellow smocks and blue surgical gloves over freshly washed hands. We would be required to do this each time we visited.

Matt was in a drug-induced coma, so we were assured he would be unaware of our presence. When we walked into his private room, I heard the clicking of the ventilator and beeping of the pumps. There was a person lying very still on the bed. I would not believe this was my son. My twenty-three year old son who was so healthy and robust lying like this, how could this happen? Matt's appearance was a shock to us. Only his face was visible, and it was bright red. His lips were grotesquely swollen. His eyelids, too, were swollen, and a tongue depressor was holding his tongue down so it would not obstruct the tubes going down his throat. I saw Nurse Alan carefully watching all of us because I'm sure he thought either I or one of Matt's sisters would faint. We held it together, but barely.

Leah, my emotional daughter, was screaming, "Matt, it's us. We love you! We love you!"

Shayna stood still and was partially hidden behind the pumps at Matt's bed. And I, well, I was dying inside. I have never felt such pain before, and I would not wish this onto my worst enemy. My knees were buckling, and Jeremy had to hold me up.

I expected Matt to sit up in bed and say, "Hi, Mom. How you doing?"

But Matt just lay still, breathing with the help of a respirator.

As we headed for the Sheraton Inn, where we were staying, I was aware of all the emotions that were running through all of us. I fell into a troubled sleep on the night of March 17, 2001. I was afraid of tomorrow, and honestly did not know how I would get through another day.

When we arrived at the burn unit the next morning, we were told that the nurses were changing Matt's dressings and we would have to wait. Once again we settled onto the floor for what seemed like a very long time. Waiting was a terrible ordeal for my family, and we were all impatient. Finally a nurse came out and told us we could come in for a few minutes. She introduced herself to us and told us she would be one of the nurses caring for Matt during the daytime shift. She said her name was Sue Mary.

We followed her into the burn unit, donned our yellow smocks and gloves, and walked into Matt's room. Once again we were reminded of the severity of Matt's injuries. We had been told by Dr. Rosenberg and Nurse Alan that it would take Matt years to recover. I did not understand that, or maybe I was in denial, because I was hoping at that moment that we could take our son and go home. I was jarred back to reality by an acrid smell that was wafting through the room. It was the smell of burned flesh, and it was coming from Matt. We were not allowed to touch Matt because of the risk of infection, but Sue Mary told me I could touch his head. I walked close to Matt's bed and pushed his hair off his forehead. My blue surgical glove was covered with gray ashes, and some of them fell onto Matt's face. I looked at Jeremy and knew he was fighting back tears. I was once again wondering how we would get through this.

We had sent Leah, Shayna, and Tricia to the cafeteria for a snack while we stayed with Matt for a few minutes. When Jeremy and I came off the elevator to join the girls, we walked into a large circle of people holding hands, our daughters and Matt's girlfriend included. Jeremy and I were introduced to an elderly gentleman named Will, who told us that his eighty-seven year old wife had just suffered a devastating stroke, and although he could not imagine losing her, he felt compelled to pray for Matt, who had his entire life ahead of him. I was very moved to know that strangers would pray for my son. Jeremy and I received a lot of hugs then, and it was the first time I had a fleeting moment of hope and felt like I would be able to get through this and give Matt the support that he would need.

Every morning we awoke to sunshine and warmth, but I still shivered and was eager to get to the burn unit. The first Monday in the unit, we met Dr. David Mozingo, the head of the burn Unit. He told us that Matt had done well over the weekend and was stable and "rock solid," a term we kept hearing throughout Matt's stay in the hospital. He had started to breathe over the ventilator, which meant that he was breathing on his own, but the machine would be kept on as a precautionary measure. We discussed with Dr. Mozingo a game plan for Matt. First, his burned skin would be removed, and a synthetic material called Integra, yes, like the little car, would be laid down. This would act as a dermis, or first layer, for the skin grafts, which would come shortly thereafter. Dr. Mozingo said once Matt was completely covered with Integra, the risk for infection would go way down and his chances for survival would go up. He would start operating the next day.

We arrived very early the next morning. Jeremy, Leah, Shayna, and I cried again as we watched the nurses wheel Matt into the operating room. While Matt was in surgery, we went to the cafeteria for some food. I realized I had not eaten anything since arriving in Florida, but I had no appetite, and I could not even force myself to eat one bite. My family started to nag me about eating, but their nagging did no good.

Once we returned to the seventh floor, we saw that there was a commotion in the hallway and knew the burn unit was admitting another patient. We met Mrs. Gray, with whom we shared the floor outside the unit, and three of her daughters. I saw myself in Mrs. Gray. She was crying and worried about her husband, who had been burned when an aerosol can exploded in his burning trash bin. His clothes had caught fire, and she had to throw a carpet on him to put out the flames.

We sat with the Gray family for a while. They told us about him. We told them about Matt. We agreed to pray for each other, and we left them to speak with Dr. Mozingo, who motioned to us that Matt was out of surgery. The doctor told us that Matt had come through his first surgery wonderfully. He tolerated the anesthesia well, and all his vital signs were normal. He would be brought back to his room shortly, and we would be able to spend time with him. In retrospect, it seems strange to say that we would spend time with Matt since he was in a drug-induced coma and most likely had no idea we were by his bedside. The doctor told us that this would be a tough time for us. We would watch Matt go through surgery and know that he was fighting for his life, and when he awoke, we would have to deal with all his emotions, plus our own.

Tricia came to Matt's room shortly after he returned from surgery, and we could tell she had been crying. She handed me a newspaper, and what I saw startled as well as scared me. It was an article written about the crash in the *Daytona Beach Daily News*. It was in color, and the top half of the front page showed a charred and smashed airplane. The headline read, "Three Survive Fiery Plane Crash." There was a photo of the paramedics putting either Phil or Francois, the pilot who was observing, on the helicopter. Once again I was crying and staring at the article. A nurse came to me and took the newspaper out of my hand. He asked to see it, and he introduced himself to us. His name was Bruce Butler. I liked Bruce immediately. He seemed competent and very conscientious, and I knew he would take good care of Matt. Jeremy, Leah, Shayna, Tricia, and I were not doing well. We kept crying, and we were very concerned and scared. Jeremy and I thought we were about to lose our son and the pain was unbearable. Dr. Mozingo told us he would give Matt a few days to recover and then it would be back to surgery to put Integra on his back. We had no idea there would be so many surgeries, but we figured this would be a long road to recovery.

After Bruce assured us Matt was all right and resting comfortably, we went to Civitan Blood Bank to donate for Matt. I have a photo of Shayna, who was the match for Matt. She was worried that they would take all her blood for Matt, and I laughed a little. Matt has B negative blood, which is quite rare, so we were told to get as much blood to the hospital as we could. Even if we did not have Matt's precious B negative type, the hospital would need and use every unit we sent them.

When we returned to the hospital, we had two visitors, two men from the FAA. One of them handed me a paper that he said was the preliminary NTSB report. Jeremy and I unfolded it and read their findings. It said that Phil turned off the right engine and the fuel selector was turned off. This was apparently done after the GUMPS check was completed (gas, undercarriage, mixture, props, switches, and seat belts), usually done on downwind with a visual approach. The airplane started to slow down, but the props were still rotating. The FAA learned that all this was done at about 700 feet when usually the fuel selector should not be turned off below 3,000 feet for normal operations or training so the pilot can recover. This airplane was too low and could not recover. Witnesses said they saw the plane clipping tree branches, and the right wing was on fire. They said it looked like the plane landed with a hard bump. One man jumped from the right side and started to run. He was on fire, and he knelt down on the ground. A young high school senior took off his jacket and had the man lie down. He then patted out the flames. The other men had exited the plane and were lying on the ground. Sirens could be heard in the distance, and paramedics reached the scene in about three minutes. That man who was on fire was Matt. I felt like I took a dozen steps backward because the thought of my child on fire was too much to handle.

Tricia was able to find out about the young man who stopped to help Matt. She learned that his name was Jonathan Shulas, and he was a high school senior on his way to an ROTC meeting. He saw the plane coming in too low, with the right wing dipping, so he pulled over and watched. When he saw Matt jump out of the plane, he ran to help. Later he told us that when he came up to Matt, he felt Matt was in shock because he was kneeling on the ground while his shirt was on fire. Jonathan pushed Matt down on the ground, took his jacket off, and began to pat the flames out. He asked Matt how many other people were on the plane and was told two. Jonathan, being assured everyone was out of the burning aircraft, turned back to Matt and sat on the ground with him until the paramedics arrived.

We were told that Roy, the head paramedic, administered to Matt. He cut off Matt's burned clothes and also cut off his new Nikes and discarded everything. He did a tracheotomy in the field and gave Matt enough morphine to put him to sleep. Matt was loaded onto the ambulance and sent to Flagler Hospital, where he stayed for about two hours. He then was put aboard a medical helicopter and was flown the seventeen minutes to Shands.

CHAPTER
THREE

The next morning, we arrived at the hospital after breakfast at the Pancake House. I still had not eaten anything, but this morning I ate one pancake half and drank a cup of tea. On the shuttle bus ride to the hospital, I felt myself getting anxious, and I wanted to see Matt. We rushed into the lobby, but I had to make a quick stop into the ladies' room, where I promptly vomited. Shayna, who was with me, ran out to tell Jeremy that "Mom is sick." That stop in the ladies' room was something that would plague me for the next three months. My stomach ached constantly, and I could not control the urge to vomit. I realized I had to get a grip on my emotions, but tell that to any mother!

At the hospital, the three girls pointed out a gift that Matt had received from some friends of ours in Los Angeles. It was a stuffed teddy bear holding a bunch of get-well balloons. The card said "feel better soon" and "thinking of you" wishes. Tricia said she wanted to make a scrapbook for Matt, so I gave her the card to start her collection. Leah was very upset that she did not have the chance to see the card that Tricia already had in her possession. An argument started between the girls because Tricia said it was just a get-well card and

Leah was not missing anything, and Leah said the card had been sent to her brother from people she knew and she had the right to see it. Jeremy and I realized at that point there was no love between these two girls, but we were not in an emotional state to be the intermediary. I was just annoyed at their childish behavior.

We decided it would be best for Leah and Shayna to fly home and return to their respective responsibilities. Leah was now working in the pharmaceutical industry, and Shayna would be graduating from high school in June. At the airport, we promised the girls we would fly home the following weekend because we had to find a house to buy and our move was coming closer.

On Monday morning, March 26, Dr. Mozingo took Matt back to surgery to examine his arms and hands. We sat in the surgery waiting room once again with the Gray family. Mr. Gray was undergoing surgery to repair his tracheostomy. Mrs. Gray and I held hands and cried together while we waited. The doctor finally came to talk to her and said everything went as expected and Mr. Gray was resting comfortably. She was so relieved.

Finally Dr. Mozingo walked into the room, but he did not have good news. He said both Matt's arms and hands were so badly burned and the injury was so severe, the only resolution would be amputation of both arms up to the elbow. The blow was too shocking, and Jeremy and I broke down. I am quite sure Dr. Mozingo did not quite know what to say to us because he told us to think about it and not make a decision yet. Even though Jeremy had been practicing medicine in the Los Angeles area for over twenty years and had a very busy internal medicine-pulmonary diseases practice, this was different. He was on the other side of the fence this time. He was Dad, not Doctor, and it was breaking his heart to see his handsome son so badly injured.

That night at the hotel, Jeremy and I sat on the edge of the bed together and cried. We did not know what to do. We were not doing anyone any good because we could not slept all night and we were both very tired and nonfunctional the next day.

Matt would be having surgery again the next morning. His back would be covered with Integra. As usual, we made our way to the waiting room to anxiously wait for Dr. Mozingo to come and talk to us. This time we brought our laptop computer with us, so we spent the time looking up everything we could find about prosthetics. There was a new myoelectric arm that was cutting-edge technology and looked like the real thing, but was it good enough? Jeremy and I talked about our dilemma again, but neither of us could make a decision and amputation was so final. What if we were making a mistake?

Dr. Mozingo finally came to talk to us and once again said there was no need to make a hasty decision. Even though Matt's arms were so badly injured, they were not hindering his recovery. And by the way, we could meet Matt on his gurney as he made his way back to his room. We walked the long corridor and saw "Big Mike" wheeling Matt to his room. Matt was sleeping, but something was different. He was off the ventilator and was breathing on his own. Big Mike, a surgical nurse, explained to us that the doctor decided to take him off the machine during surgery, and because Matt continued to breathe peacefully on his own, he was taken off the breathing device. I was so excited. I mistakenly equated this with recovery, but I did not realize that our path down this road with Matt was just beginning.

When we were able to come into Matt's room, we were greeted by Sue Mary and Jody, who were taking care of him that day. Even though he still had Ativan and morphine in his system and seemed to be fast asleep, he was moving around a bit and ended up on his right side. We noticed that he was not closing his eyes properly, and his eyelids appeared to be pulling together.

Jody was adjusting his blanket and remarked, "Mrs. Cole, your son has beautiful blue eyes."

Jeremy and I jumped up and said, "You mean brown."

She said, "No, blue."

Well, Matt did not have blue eyes. They were dark brown exactly like mine.

Jeremy checked Matt's eyes and said to Sue Mary, "We need an ophthalmology consult. It looks like he's getting an infection."

Sue Mary immediately called the Ophthalmology department, and probably within an hour, the doctor came, followed by his entourage of residents and fellows. On examination, he could see that Matt had a severe fungus infection and would need to be treated. A course of antibiotic ointments and anti-fungal salves was prescribed and had to be administered every fifteen minutes. I was glad Matt was asleep because I do not think he would have been able to tolerate all the jelly-like materials that were squeezed into his eyes.

We had now been in Gainesville for two weeks, and we were scheduled to fly home that afternoon. Sue Mary said that Matt's oxygen saturation had dropped drastically, and he would be taken to Radiology for a CAT scan because it was possible he had suffered some sort of neurological event and there was brain damage. I was hysterical and told Jeremy I would not go home. He said to give it a few hours and see how Matt does.

In about three hours, we learned that Matt's brain waves were more active and he was sleeping comfortably. There appeared to be no brain damage. Now I could go home and look for a house.

We left Tricia with Matt, and we made our way to the airport. At LAX, we were met by our daughters. The four of us fell into each other's arms and cried again. At that moment, my stomach was hurting, and I was frightened we would never be normal again. Life as we knew it had changed drastically, and I found myself wishing I knew how to turn back the clock.

Leah drove with Shayna in the front, and Jeremy and I were in the back seat. We were all quiet on the drive to the San Fernando Valley. Leah said that she and Shayna had a surprise for us at our house. Our ride took about thirty minutes, and when we walked into our kitchen, we had another shock. Our entire house had been packed, and everything had been organized and stacked neatly into boxes. Leah had arranged for our friends to come to our house that morning and pack. The girls supplied all the deli food everyone could eat, my friend Sona kept the coffee brewing, and everyone packed. Now I really had to find a place to live, and quickly!

CHAPTER
FOUR

We were having difficulty thinking about buying a house. We did not know what we wanted and could not seem to make a decision. We spoke to our real estate lady, and she said, "How about renting?"

What a great idea. The next day she took me to see about three houses that were for rent. I really liked one of them so we signed all the papers, put down the security deposit and first and last month's rent, and we were ready to go.

The next day, I arranged for the moving truck and had all the utilities transferred. We would move in two days. During the course of the day, Jeremy or I would call the hospital to check on Matt, and I would talk to Tricia. I was planning to return to Gainesville on Saturday, and Tricia would return to her job as a flight attendant on Monday.

Our move went smoothly, and we were settling into our rental house. We had signed a one-year lease but figured we would be there for a while since we had no idea how long Matt would be in the hospital. Right then our futures seemed uncertain, but I liked thinking about bringing Matt home, and positive thoughts about him kept me going.

Saturday was bright and full of sunshine the first part of April. My family took me to the airport, and we cried again. We seemed to be doing that a lot, but we did not know when we would see each other. That was a sad moment to leave my daughters behind with my husband, but we felt Matt needed support and Mom would be the best person to give him whatever he might need.

Tricia met me at the airport, and even though it was evening, I had to go to see Matt. When we walked into the unit, we saw Bruce, who was in charge this evening. He said Matt had been resting and his vital signs were "rock solid." To me, Matt looked thinner, but I was told he was still weighing in at a hearty 118 pounds. Bruce also told me that a hand surgeon would be in the unit at 11:00 a.m. tomorrow to talk to me about starting hand reconstruction.

Tricia and I arrived on time and met a Dr. Caffey who was the head of the Hand and Plastics Department at the hospital. He told us that he and Dr. Mozingo discussed Matt's case, and he wanted to try to save Matt's hands. That sounded just fine to me. He told me he would cut slits in Matt's groin and bury his hands in the slits. They would stay buried for about three weeks. Again, I was thankful that Matt was asleep. I was starting to understand what Dr. Mozingo meant when he said our family would go through the emotions twice. Every time I spoke to a doctor, my stomach ached and my heart pounded, and now I knew I would have to go through all this again with Matt when I explained everything to him.

The surgery was scheduled for Monday morning, but Sunday evening was moving day again. I moved into the apartment I would live in while Matt was in the hospital. We went to the hotel to gather our belongings, but both Tricia and I only had two small suitcases. The apartment was furnished and had everything we would need. Tricia would live with me about fifty percent of the time, and the rest of the time she would be at work with Delta Airlines. I would drive her car, and she would drive Matt's little Acura Integra.

The next morning I hugged Tricia as she left for work, and I hurried to the hospital so I could see Matt before he was taken to surgery. When I arrived in his room, there was a lady who was standing close to his bed and was typing on her laptop.

When she saw me, she very arrogantly said, "Excuse me. We're busy here!"

I was taken aback by her attitude, and by now I had plenty of my own attitude, so I said, "Excuse me. I'm his mother. And you are?"

She did not answer me. She just packed up her computer and walked out. Sue Mary told me she was the workers' compensation agent. I did not even think about workers' comp because we had private health insurance and I assumed that would be the help we would need to pay for Matt's medical bills.

Before Matt was taken to surgery, the doctors made sure I understood what they would be doing in the operating room. I was very frightened and concerned while watching the nurses wheel Matt down the long corridor, but once again I made my way to the family waiting room. I had a book with me, but as usual, I got no reading done because I could not concentrate. This surgery took a long time, and after waiting for over three hours, I really became scared. Finally, about four hours later, the doctor came to talk to me. He said the operation went smoothly, but because Matt was so thin, he had difficulty burying Matt's hands in his bony groin. Matt's hands would stay in these flaps for about three weeks. The doctor reminded me of the severity of the injury, and he said he had no idea what he would find after three weeks. The reason for the surgery was to grow healthy tissue on the hands, but with the compromised blood supply in the hands, he did not know if any new tissue would grow. Only time would tell.

When I returned to Matt's room and saw that he was sleeping very peacefully, I sat down in the easy chair with a heavy heart. I was not seated long when I heard screaming coming from the hall. I walked outside the room and learned, to my dismay, that Mr. Gray had just died. Mrs. Gray was not taking it well, and I could feel her pain. Mr. Gray was hypertensive, diabetic, and overweight, all the risk factors that made it almost impossible for him to survive, but it was heartbreaking, nonetheless. Mrs. Gray hugged me and told me she would continue to pray for Matt, and she asked me to pray for the soul of her dear husband. I felt very lonely at the moment. I missed my husband and daughters who were in Los Angeles, I missed

Tricia, who was at work, and most of all, I missed Matt because he was in a coma. Once again I wondered how I would get through this and would I be strong enough to help Matt get through this most difficult time in his life.

It was now mid-April, and Matt had been in the hospital for a month. He had been through twelve operations, and Sue Mary said 98 percent of his grafts had taken and were healing nicely. She also said that Matt's face would heal because it looked like his burns were second degree and not third. His eye infection was healing, but Dr. Mozingo said soon he would start to reconstruct Matt's eyelids since they were healing and shrinking in the process. Closing his eyes properly was not possible, and therefore he would have ongoing infections. This needed to be fixed as soon as possible.

At home, in my apartment I made myself a cup of soup and sat down to watch the news. I had no idea what was going on in the world. I promptly fell asleep with the TV on and woke up the next morning at six. My soup remained untouched. It was now time to get ready for another day in the burn unit. Matt was scheduled for surgery in the morning, and we would have visitors arriving in the late afternoon.

Tricia came home from her four-day work trip and drove the hour and a half from Orlando, where she was based, to Gainesville. She quickly said hello to Matt and blew air kisses at him since we were not allowed to touch or kiss him yet.

She and I left to pick up Leah and Matt's friend, David Moss, from San Diego. Longtime friends from Los Angeles, R. J. Schlanger and Shanen Whalen, had flown into Jacksonville and would drive up to Gainesville. We expected them shortly.

When we came back to the hospital, Leah was shocked to see Matt. Since she had last seen him, he was off the ventilator, his swollen lips had gone down considerably, and he looked like he was sleeping peacefully. Of course, Leah cried and cried and was inconsolable. She said she wanted her brother back. I said I wanted my son back, and the two of us fell apart. The nurse taking care of Matt that night was a man named Keith Carpenter. He, too, was very caring and competent, and I knew he took excellent care of Matt. When he would be on duty during the night, along with Bruce Butler and Jason Williams, whom we always called Yard Dog, but I no longer remember how that started, I always would sleep well because I knew Matt was in very capable bands.

Matt's three friends came to the unit later in the evening, and it was interesting to see their reaction when they saw Matt. Shanen, the group clown and prankster, was quiet. R. J. had to walk out of the room, and David was very somber. The boys brought Matt a CD player along with some of what they thought would be his favorite CDs. They played Kenny G over and over. I thought I would go nuts. I do like Kenny G, but some of the musical pieces were quite depressing.

Finally after two or three days, the boys headed for California. Shanen and R. J. drove back to Jacksonville for their flight back to LAX. David went to the Gainesville airport to catch his flight to San Diego. Leah would stay with me through the weekend.

I noticed that Matt's blood pressure was really low and his face and lips were very pale. I mentioned this to Bruce, who promised to check Matt. His blood pressure was dropping very quickly, and when it read sixty-five over fifty-two I became really frightened. Bruce called for the doctors. A Dr. Gallagher came with the usual residents behind him. We were asked to step out of the room.

Leah was hysterical and told Bruce, "Don't let my brother die! Take good care of Matt!"

Tricia was silent, and I was fighting the worst pain I have ever felt in my life. I thought Matt was dying. I knew he had one of the infections that burn patients are susceptible to, but I did not know which one he was fighting.

We three girls went outside and found a bench to sit on. Tricia decided she would look for four-leaf clovers, and Leah and I continued to sit there not moving or speaking. We stayed outside for about an hour. When we went back in, we bumped into David. His flight had been cancelled, and he would fly out in the morning. He wanted to know what happened because he was not allowed back in the burn unit, and he said there was a lot of activity around Matt's room. We had no answers.

When we got back to the seventh floor, we were buzzed in, and Leah and Tricia were holding me up. I was waiting for one of the nurses or Dr. Gallagher to tell me that they had done everything they could for Matt, but they had lost him. I was terrified, and I was not breathing.

Bruce came out of Matt's room, and he said, "There you are! Matt's fine. Come on in!"

Leah, Tricia, and I were so relieved we threw ourselves at Bruce and were hugging him and mumbling our thanks. Poor Bruce. He was so patient with us.

That night, Jeremy called and asked if I could pick him up at the airport.

"What airport?" I asked.

He was in Gainesville to see Matt. One of the residents had called to speak with him, and he was so concerned he rescheduled all his patients, signed out to a colleague, and was on the first flight he could find to Atlanta. He knew if he told me be was flying to Gainesville, I would have gone off the deep end. He knew me too well.

The next morning, we took David to the airport and saw his plane take off for Atlanta. He was on the first leg back to San Diego. Tricia left for work again, and Leah was still in town with us. We went back to my apartment and made coffee and had a bowl of cereal. After freshening up a bit, we drove to the hospital. We were greeted by Sue Mary and Jody, who were taking care of Matt. They told us that Matt had been septic from a tainted central line that went into his groin. The line was changed, and now Matt was recovering. His hands were still in their flaps and the operation to start repairing his eyelids was scheduled for tomorrow.

Jeremy and Leah stayed with me in Gainesville until the weekend, and when Jeremy was sure Matt was no longer in danger, he left for home.

Matt's eyelid surgery went well, but we were shocked to see his appearance when he returned to his room. His hair had been shaved off, and skin from his scalp was used to build a new eyelid. Both Matt's eyes were sewn shut with bright blue thread, and a yellow wad of cotton or sponge, called a bolster, covered each eye.

He looked awful, but at least he was sleeping and had no idea what was happening.

Within five days, the bolsters were removed, and the stitches were taken out from around Matt's eyes. They looked so much better, and, hopefully, we would abort any future eye infections since Matt's eyes were completely closing. We also noticed, when the ophthalmologist pointed it out, Matt's eyes were now back to his original brown color.

Sue Mary loved to remove staples. Every day when she and Jody took care of Matt, he would look great. They would clean him up, and Sue Mary would pull all the staples out from around the new grafts. She was so excited to see how well Matt was healing, and she showed me Matt's legs, which had not been burned but were used for donor sites. His poor, skinny legs were red, raw, and oozing. She said this would give him more problems than the third degree burns. How right she was!

May was just a couple of days away, and I fell into what I called my Gainesville routine.

I would get up every morning and make coffee. I would then prepare for the day. I always made sure I wore some makeup and applied concealer to the dark circles that were present under my eyes. I would not be allowed into the burn unit until 11:00 a.m. after Matt had had his bath and his dressings changed. I was still battling the ubiquitous stomachache, and I noticed I had lost weight because my pants were falling down. I would always ask Miss Joyce at the nurse's desk for a safety pin so I could pull my pants tighter. She kept telling me I should eat more.

In retrospect, I realize I was no help to the nurses in the unit. I do not think I was expected to be, but I was always there, and it gave me great comfort to stroke Matt's forehead and to hear him breathe. It had been a long six weeks in the burn unit, and I saw no end in sight. I missed my family. Jeremy, Leah, and Shayna were always on my mind, and I missed talking to my son. I missed his smile and his sense of humor. I missed seeing what a wonderful young man he had become. I prayed that one day we would leave the burn unit and get back to our life in California, but for now I would just have to be patient.

CHAPTER
FIVE

Matt loved to fly. His goal was to one day fly the heavy iron. He had earned his private pilot's license when he was seventeen. The day after he came home with his license, he invited me to go for a ride when his school day ended. In our area of Los Angeles, seniors only went to school in the morning, so I met Matt at Van Nuys Airport at noon. I watched him prepare the plane for flight. He was crawling under the plane and checking the brake pads and the landing gear, the hydraulic system, and the tires. I climbed into the plane after Matt and adjusted my headsets. I was very excited but a bit apprehensive, also, since I realized my life was now in the hands of my seventeen-year-old son. We were in a single-engine Piper Cherokee with the tail number November 8231 Tango.

It was a beautiful day in January 1995. Matt talked to the tower, and before I knew it, we were off the ground. We flew north along the beautiful coast of California, and Matt told me we would stop in Santa Barbara for lunch and then return to Van Nuys.

I was thoroughly enjoying my flight. To the east, I could see the rugged mountains, and beneath me, the Pacific was a crystal blue. I had been so wrapped up in the beautiful scenery that I was unaware of the silence. I did not hear any air traffic calls on the radio, nor did I hear other flights talking. I asked Matt what was going on, and he said, "Nothing." I went back to the scenery. As I looked ahead, I could see what I thought was a runway. It also seemed that our plane was descending. I asked Matt if we were landing, and if we were, who told us we could do that. His exact words were, "Mom, right now I'm gonna land this puppy!"

We landed safely, and Matt taxied to an empty space where we parked the plane. Matt told me we had lost the radio and had had no contact with the tower. He had squawked an emergency, and the tower got everyone out of our way. After we landed, those who were coming into Santa Barbara were allowed to land.

All this excitement had occurred and I missed it. Matt was so calm and proficient that I never knew we were in trouble.

After his graduation from high school, Matt decided on Pierce College in Woodland Hills. This was a community college, and his dad and I felt that was a good way for him to start. He was also working for a videography company. He would travel to ice skating competitions around Southern California, and he would videotape the competitors. Even though he only worked weekends, he loved what he was doing, and the money was good for a teenager.

About six months into his career as a videographer, he told us that the two owners were drinking a lot, probably doing drugs, and were starting to miss events. Matt now often went to competitions by himself and would film all the ice-skaters alone. We advised Matt to talk to the owners and find out what they were planning. It turned out they had no plans. As a matter of fact, they were not even interested in the business. They told Matt he could take it over and have all the equipment since it was used and not in the greatest condition.

Matt and his dad drove to North Hollywood to pick up all the video equipment and brought it home and put it in our garage. Now he had to schedule work, but that was no problem either. He was booked every weekend for six months in advance.

The first thing Matt did was rename the company Competition Video. He organized all the skaters' tapes and recorded their orders from the master tape. Then he delivered the finished tapes to the skaters and their parents. Everyone seemed thrilled to finally be receiving their videotapes.

Matt continued his routine of taking classes at Pierce College and working every weekend. By now he had traded in his Acura Integra and had bought the newer model, and he seemed to be enjoying life, but I sensed he wanted more. Even though he continued to fly in the Piper and was now taking instrument lessons with an instructor named Alan Goldsman, I knew he was thinking about the big planes that he loved and dreamed about.

Sure enough, in early January 1999, he ran into the kitchen and said, "Mom, check this out. I got accepted!"

He was talking about his acceptance to Flight Safety International in Vero Beach, Florida. He was so excited to be pursuing his career in aviation, and we were thrilled and very proud of our son.

During the month, Matt was busy delegating positions to people who would take over Competition Video. First on his list would be his sister, Leah, and her friend Elizabeth. They would do the scheduling and taping from the master tape and talking to the parents. Matt was diligently looking to hire a cameraman. He found someone, and the man came over and brought his brag book with him. He told us he had worked for the movie industry for a long time, knew everything there was to know about cameras, and he certainly was the man for the job. Matt hired him.

At the next competition, with Leah in charge, this master cameraman showed up, along with all his bravado, and taped the ice. He missed every skating routine, every skater, and basically did not record anything but the floor. Parents were angry, tempers were flaring, and everyone was taking it out on Leah. They made no money that weekend, no one got paid, and this guy was out on his ear. Leah would have to go back to the drawing board and start looking for a competent cameraman.

On January 22, 1999 Matt packed his Integra with his clothes, his humidor with his favorite cigars, and his stereo system and CDs, and he and I were on our way to Vero Beach, Florida. Matt's flight classes would begin on February first.

I had called the school ahead and had arranged for Matt to move into the dorms at Flight Safety. I gave Dennis, who was in charge of the men's dorm, my credit card, and he assured me there would be a bed for Matt when we arrived.

We made our way to Florida from California along the I-10. We drove through Tucson, Houston, and New Orleans, where we stopped for a scrumptious dinner and heard really great jazz. Our trip was uneventful, but Matt was anxious to get to Florida. He could not wait to start school. I say school because in addition to flying and learning the technology of the airplane, he would be required to attend ground school classes and be in an actual classroom setting.

When we arrived at the dorm, Dennis was waiting for us. He gave us a tour of the school and then he took us back to what would be Matt's room. We unlocked the door and walked into the room. We met the first roommate, Karl, who was from Germany and was busy cooking cabbage and bratwurst, with a cigarette hanging from his mouth.

I thought, *Oh boy. This will be good!*

We unpacked Matt's belongings and then went out for dinner. Karl declined our invitation because he already had a feast prepared for himself. I stayed in town for one day, and Matt and I watched our Los Angeles Dodgers practicing and getting ready for the upcoming season. We then headed for the Orlando airport, where I would board a plane back to Los Angeles, and Matt would return to Vero Beach, where a new life awaited him.

It was tough to say goodbye to Matt because he and I are really close and I knew I would miss him terribly, but I knew this was the best thing for him. It was time for him to grow up.

Back in Los Angeles, Leah was trying to make a go of Competition Video, but it was not working. She hired a new cameraman, but the morning of the competition, he was three hours late. On top of that, the lady who had originally owned the video company with her late husband reprimanded Leah for not setting up a rickety elevated platform for the cameraman to stand on. Leah had no idea that the truck it was in had been stolen, recovered, and impounded by the police. Leah was doing a great job trying to keep the company going for her brother, but it was not working. Cameramen are falling over each other in Los Angeles, but it looked like all their reputations preceded them, and they all wanted to be paid more than they were worth.

Leah and Matt discussed the situation, and Leah told her brother she was doing her best and would like to continue with the company. Matt, as sensitive as ever, said his videography company was not that important. What was important, he said, was her education. She was in her third year at USC (University of Southern California), and she must finish and do it well. He said to give the equipment and all the master tapes to another videography company who was the local competition. The man who came to pick up all the goods was impressed at how organized everything was. That was both Matt's and Leah's modus operandi. They are both compulsive and take a lot of pride in their work.

In Vero Beach, Matt was working hard at earning his instrument license. He told us that he had scored a one hundred percent on his written test. His dad and I were shocked. This was a kid who could not pass a test to save himself, and he was excelling in flight school. I guess he had found his passion.

We would speak to Matt on the phone at least once or twice a week. After he earned his instrument license, he started working on his CFI or Certified Flight Instructor license, but he mentioned one time that he was not feeling well. He said he had a constant low-grade headache and his nose was stuffy all the time. To me, it sounded like he had developed some Florida allergies. Jeremy concurred, but said Matt's allergies were due to secondhand smoke. Both of Matt's roommates, Karl from Germany and Karl from Sweden, were smokers. Jeremy's assessment made sense to me, but now we had to find a solution.

Jeremy and I discussed this problem and decided it was time for Matt to get his own apartment. When I called Matt the next day to tell him to start looking, he was thrilled. He said he hoped he had proven to us that he was trustworthy and mature enough to take care of himself. He thanked me profusely for the opportunity to have his own apartment. He knew his dad and I would be funding the operation, and he assured me we would not have to worry.

He found a one-bedroom apartment near the beach, and he faxed the contract to his dad to peruse and make the final decision. Everything looked fine to us, so we gave Matt the green light, and he signed the one-year lease.

Unfortunately, Matt had no furniture in Vero Beach, so he flew home and we rented a U-Haul. In it he put all his bedroom furniture, and I gave him a chair from our family room. We then went to Target, where I bought him a set of dishes, a set of silverware, a frying pan, a blender, a two-cup coffeepot, and some other kitchen odds and ends. As he followed me around the store, he kept asking, "What do I need this for?" I asked him if he expected to have a steady diet of McDonald's and Burger King. He said, "Good point." He then said we forgot the can opener so we had better go back to the gadgets aisle to pick one up.

We carefully packed everything in the U-Haul and once again, headed east on the I-10 Interstate.

Our four-day trip took us into Jacksonville, where we picked up the I-95 and drove the four-hour trip south to Vero Beach. At first glimpse, I thought Matt's new apartment was a dump, but he was so excited, I said nothing. We started to unload the truck when a handsome young man came out of the apartment across the grassy area from Matt's. He introduced himself and said he, too, was attending Flight Safety International. What a small world! Thankfully, he helped Matt unload some of the bigger pieces of furniture, so I busied myself in the kitchen. We invited him to go for dinner with us, but he declined saying his parents were in town and he would be joining them.

I left for Los Angeles the next day and felt better knowing Matt had a friend in his complex. As it turned out, Matt was two licenses ahead of that fellow and they would study together.

Everything was going along smoothly. Matt was studying hard, doing well academically, and flying mostly every day, Florida weather permitting.

In mid-September, he informed us that he had met a girl. Her name was Carol, and she lived in an apartment somewhere in the complex with her mother. Jeremy and I were thrilled that he had someone to go to the movies and the beach with and, of course, someone to socialize with.

We had hoped that Matt would come home for Thanksgiving, but as it turned out, Matt had a flight the next day, and the cross-country flight was too long to be home for just a day. It was a bittersweet holiday without Matt. His dad, his sisters, and I missed him terribly, but we would see him the first week of December. Jeremy and I decided to bring Thanksgiving to him in Florida, but I refused to carry a turkey in my suitcase. All supplies would have to be bought in Vero Beach, and if the traditional foods were unavailable, then I would improvise.

We flew into Orlando, rented a car, and drove into Vero Beach. We had not seen Matt since September, and he was very excited to have us visit. We had a wonderful day together, and we met Carol. She was not what I expected her to be. She was quite short and rather chubby, but she had a contagious smile, and her blue eyes sparkled when she spoke. She loved to laugh, and she was smitten with Matt. I admired her good taste in men, and her relationship with my son was fine with me.

On Saturday of that weekend, we rented a multi-engine Seminole, and Matt took us on a flight. He was now rated in instruments and multi-engines, so we felt confident he would give us a great, and safe, ride. We flew to Naples, where we had dinner at a delicious BBQ restaurant. Two or three times, Carol excused herself to go outdoors to smoke. We were surprised that Matt would be involved with a smoker, considering how strongly we feel about the dangers of smoking. The flag was going up, but Jeremy and I kept quiet.

On Sunday. I prepared my après-Thanksgiving feast. I had found a turkey with all the trimmings at a local store, so I was busy in the kitchen all day. We would be joined by Matt's friend, Sam, who was attending Flight Safety from India. He was a long way from home, so we especially enjoyed having him for dinner. Carol informed me that her mother would not be joining us, either, because she was hung over from the previous night. I was now worried about the role models Carol had. She told me the previous night that her mother was presently between husbands and she had recently divorced husband number four. Her grandmother, who also lived in Vero Beach, was in the process of divorcing husband number seven. This was not looking good.

We had a wonderful dinner and celebrated the upcoming holiday season. For us, Hanukkah came early that year, so Jeremy, Matt, and I lit the first candle on Matt's Chanukiot, and we had presents for all the kids. Matt got a new jacket, Carol a beaded bracelet that was so popular then, and Sam got a gift certificate to a local music store.

We would be headed for Los Angeles on Sunday in the late afternoon, so Jeremy and I found a little restaurant along the boardwalk where we had breakfast while Matt had a spin lesson. As we walked along the beach, I purposely kept my head down. I did not want to see a small plane spinning to the ground, and this was the first and only time I was nervous about Matt's training.

Once again it was so tough to leave Matt in Vero Beach as we headed back to Los Angeles because we missed him terribly, but it was thrilling to see what an amazing young man Matt was becoming. And his passion for flying was staggering. It was obvious to us that he lived to fly and he could not wait to start his day in an airplane.

In Los Angeles, we celebrated the remainder of Hannukah with Leah, Shayna, and our dear friends, the Rosenbergs, and we enjoyed potato latkes and exchanged gifts. Even though we were having a wonderful time with family and friends, I could hear Matt's laughter in my head. He was always present even though he was three thousand miles away.

For the next three months, Matt continued his training as well as his relationship with Carol. Everything seemed to be going well. In February 2000, our family decided to go to Solitude, Utah, to ski. Since Matt had completed his MEI, or multi-engine instructor license, he had decided to move to Daytona Beach to resume school at Embry-Riddle Aeronautical University, and he had a job lined up at one of the local FBOs, or fixed base operations, as a flight instructor. To our family, education is the most important thing you can have, and we were overjoyed that Matt would continue classes and earn credits toward his degree. There was one problem. Carol wanted to move to Daytona Beach with Matt. Conservative Matt did not think this would be a good idea so soon. He wanted to move, settle into an apartment, and have her move out later. Carol did not like this idea, and when Matt went to pick her up in the evening from work, she was nowhere around. Matt told us that she had met someone new in the restaurant where she worked, climbed into bed with that guy, and Matt was history. Now I realize this news is hearsay, but I am just repeating what Matt told us, and I am sure he knew what was going on.

We picked Matt up in Salt Lake City, and it was obvious he was distraught. I hated seeing him so sad, and I wondered if our yearly ski trip would be successful. We skied at Solitude and Brighton, but as much as Matt loved to ski, it was obvious his heart was not in it. He was maudlin and quiet, and I feared be was not enjoying himself. It was our family tradition to ski every year, and we all loved spending time on the slopes. I had hoped this year would be the same.

Matt and Shayna skied together, but Shayna said her brother was boring. She had never said a derogatory word about Matt. In fact, she adored her older brother. Jeremy and I took Matt aside and asked him to talk to us. His statement was plain and simple. He had fallen hard, and he missed Carol. We told him to take it slowly and maybe things would work out. He said he did not think so. I think he knew more than he was telling us.

We drove home to Los Angeles, and Matt surprised us by saying he wanted to come with us. He had nothing pressing in Daytona Beach, classes started in ten days, and he had no flight students waiting for him. He wondered if he could spend some time with us in Tarzana. Was he kidding? Matt is one of the three apples of our eye, and he was welcome any time he wanted. Shayna was ecstatic that her big bro would accompany us home, and Leah, who was recovering from an emergency appendectomy and did not ski with us, was thrilled that Matt could be home for a week or so.

When we walked into our house, we were greeted by Leah and the excitement of our three Labs. We had an assortment of retrievers: one golden, one black, and one yellow/boxer mix. Matt got down on the floor, and the dogs were all over him. I can hear him laughing and saying, "Easy does it, Molly!" She was our seventy-pound black

Lab who lived life with great gusto. Her kisses and slurping were the same. To hear Matt's laughter and playful voice, joined by his sisters, was music to my ears. The kids were now about twenty-two, twenty-one, and seventeen, but they were still kids having a good time with their dogs. Jeremy looked over everyone's heads and winked at me. We knew Matt would be all right.

We, once again, sent Matt back to Florida with a check for his rent, for food, and for whatever he might need, and we felt confident that he was taking good care of himself.

Matt was enrolled in a math class and an English class at Embry-Riddle, and he had his first student, Julius from Philadelphia, a young black man who, like Matt, wanted to fly. I knew the English class would be no problem for Matt, but I sure was worried about the math. We would have to wait and see.

There were no earth-shattering events for the next three months. I really liked the status quo of our family. The girls were doing well, also. Shayna was finishing eleventh grade and looking forward to being a senior, and Leah was set to graduate from USC in May with a bachelor of science in psychology. Life was good. I had learned over the years that if things were going smoothly for all three kids at the same time, we were in superb shape.

Matt had always been very supportive of every one of his family members. After Thursday classes in mid-May, he flew home to attend Leah's early morning graduation the next day. Of course, the Los Angeles traffic was awful even at seven in the morning. All parking lots at USC were full, and we had to park what seemed like miles away. We were faced with a long walk, and my dear husband was experiencing back problems and was scheduled for surgery the next week. Matt carried a folding chair for his dad and would stop every few feet to help Jeremy sit down for a moment.

The graduation was endless and chaotic. We never saw Leah march in, we never saw her walk up on stage to receive her diploma, and we never even heard her name called. We just sat there. Leah's friend from New York, Siobhan, had flown in, and I kept asking her if she could see anything. Finally, next to me Matt was hugging Leah and congratulating her, and all the kids were surrounding her and cheering for her. We finally got to see our graduate. Now we had to trek back to the car. Matt offered to have us wait while he went to get the car, but we all thought it would be better to stick together. There were just too many people.

That evening we had a grand celebration in Leah's honor at one of our favorite Woodland Hills restaurants. We ate delicious food and danced the hora and had a wonderful time. It was so much fun to watch Leah and her friends partying, but early next morning Jeremy would take Matt to LAX for his return to Florida and everything would be quiet in our household once again.

At the end of her school year, Shayna said to me, "Mom, let's take a trip."

I said, "Where do you want to go?"

She said, "Let's drive to Florida to see Matt."

She did not have to ask me twice. Matt said by all means come visit and see his new Daytona Beach apartment. So we loaded up the car with our suitcases and gifts for Matt's July first birthday, and once again we were on the I-10 heading east. Shayna and I stopped in Las Vegas, where we rode the roller coaster at Stateline and saw David Copperfield's Magic Show. Then we traveled on and stopped in Arlington, Texas, where we rode every roller coaster we could fit into our one-day visit to Six Flags over Texas. We then continued through New Orleans, where Shayna had her first taste of chicory coffee, and on into Florida, where we drove south on the I-95 into Daytona Beach. Matt gave us directions to his apartment, and we arrived in his parking lot on Bent Tree Drive late in the evening. He greeted us warmly and said, "Where's my cake?"

It was his twenty-third birthday, but it did not occur to me to transport a cake in my trunk in the heat of late June. What was he thinking? Shayna and I gave him his presents, and I promised to make him a chocolate cake the next day.

Jeremy and I previously bought Matt a bed-in-a-minute for occasions such as this. Shayna and I would be sleeping in great splendor in Matt's living room. As usual, I fell into a deep sleep the minute my head hit the pillow. I was awakened in the morning by some sort of prodding in the ribs. Shayna was poking me and saying, "Mom, Mom. Wake up. What's that noise?"

I could see sunshine through the blinds, so I knew it was morning, but I had no idea what that strange noise was, either.

Shayna and I took turns in the bathroom, and I went into the kitchen to look for morning coffee materials. Shayna sat at the table, and we continued to discuss the noise.

"Could be," Shayna said, "the air conditioner."

"Or the water heater," I added.

Matt must have heard us because he sauntered into the kitchen wrapped in his new birthday bathrobe.

"Girls, girls," he said. "The mystery is over. We're right by the track, and there's a race today!"

"What track? What race?" Shayna and I echoed.

"We're only a mile from the Daytona Beach race track."

Of course. But who knew? Certainly not us. The three of us sat at the table with our morning coffee and could not stop laughing. The noise continued throughout the day. I was glad to do errands so I could get away from it for a few moments.

Matt directed Shayna and me to the nearest Walmart. He really wanted his chocolate birthday cake, and I had to shop for the ingredients.

Inside the store, I was completely overwhelmed. Walmarts were not around in Southern California, and other than Costco, I had never seen anything like this. We found everything we needed for the cake, but, of course, I had to buy nine-inch cake pans, a mixer, and measuring cups. Matt did not have a fully equipped kitchen, but little by little, I was adding to it.

We made our way back to the apartment, and I started preparing for an afternoon of baking. Shayna wanted to read her book, and Matt said he was going to work for a while. Julius was coming in for a flight lesson. And first there would be an hour or so of ground school.

Once the cake was in the oven, Shayna and I went to the pool. She was swimming in the pool and I was reading my book when she said, "Hey, Mom, look, someone must be barbequing!"

The sky above us was full of smoke. Those were some hot dogs and hamburgers on the grill! I told Shayna we would keep an eye on all the smoke. As time wore on, we felt the sky was getting blacker with smoke and there was a lot of activity around the pool. One of the apartment complex managers came to tell us we had better get ready to evacuate. There was a grass fire behind the complex, and it was spreading fast and coming close to a few of the buildings. We dashed for Matt's apartment, where I put the cake on a cooling rack and wondered what belongings of Matt's I should put in the car before Shayna and I leave. We were able to track down Matt and tell him what was happening. He said he would postpone taking off with Julius, so wait for him before we leave. By the time he arrived, firefighters had the fire controlled and no one had to evacuate. We were so lucky. Now I could relax and make frosting. Chocolate, of course.

In the evening, Matt invited his friend Patrick Hyndman (whom we have always called Paddy) over, and we had a fun time eating and listening to Paddy as he regaled us with stories about his native Canada.

Shayna and I stayed with Matt during the week and enjoyed our time with him and all his new friends who would come to visit.

Toward the end of our stay, Matt invited us to the Daytona Beach Ice Rink for a hockey game. Matt was the goaltender, and it amazed me how my little five-foot-seven-inch son could be so proficient at catching a thirty-five-mile-per-hour puck as it flew toward him. We met all his hockey buddies, including a Continental Airlines pilot and a local radiologist. The guys told me that at pickup games, every team wanted Matt to be their goalie. To this day, he is an avid hockey fan, and I know he dreams about one day playing again.

After an exciting Saturday at Busch Gardens in Tampa, Shayna and I headed for home. On our lengthy ride home, Shayna was already saying she missed her brother, but we would all rendezvous in New York City at the end of July for a family wedding.

Life at home in Tarzana was quiet, as usual. Leah had found a job with a pharmaceutical company and had started to work close to home in the San Fernando Valley, and Shayna resumed her summer job at a local flower shop where she sold bouquets and arrangements, and also learned how to make a floral centerpiece.

Plans were being made to fly to New York City to attend my cousin Tamara's wedding. The four of us would fly from Los Angeles to La Guardia, and Matt would come from Orlando to New York, and we would all participate in the family festivities. Flights were arranged, my girls were busily deciding what dresses to wear, Jeremy's patient schedule was changed and covered, and we were on our way.

We had an exceptionally bumpy flight to New York and were greeted with thunderstorms and flooding once we landed. As we settled into our rooms at the beautiful Waldorf Astoria, we were all talking about getting together with family and looking forward to the good time we would have. Matt would be on his way from Orlando shortly, and Leah's friend Siobhan would pick him up at the airport, since she lived so close to La Guardia, and would drive him to the hotel where we would all have dinner.

Siobhan waited at the airport for about three hours. She finally called us with the bad news she had just received; because of bad weather all along the eastern seaboard, Matt's flight had been cancelled. In fact, all flights coming into New York from Orlando were cancelled and not being rescheduled. We were very upset, to say the least, but, of course, I was grateful that the airlines were taking no chances by letting all those planes fly into thunderstorms. We would have to see Matt another time, and as long as we were already in New York, we would have a nice time.

Having spent the weekend with family and celebrating with them, Jeremy, the girls, and I flew back to Los Angeles on Sunday. We were now getting excited about our late August family cruise. Once again, we would attempt to meet with Matt, this time in Fort Lauderdale. We hoped that everything would go smoothly and we would all enjoy our family vacation.

We left for Florida on Friday August eighteenth, Matt planned to drive from Daytona Beach to Fort Lauderdale, and we would all meet at our hotel. But first things first, Matt was taking his math final in the early afternoon, and immediately after that he had a flight.

We had dinner at our hotel and then went up to our suite to watch movies and wait for Matt and Siobhan, who was also joining us on the cruise. At midnight we heard a knock on the door. Leah and Shayna flew off the couch and onto the back of whoever was on the other side of the door. Jeremy and I knew Matt had arrived and was being wildly greeted by his sisters. He looked somehow more grown-up than he did a month ago, and he seemed much more confident and sure of himself.

After the girls finally settled down, with Siobhan in the room with them, and went to sleep, Matt came into our portion of the suite to talk. He was concerned about his math final. He said he had worked really hard, but the teacher was not a very patient fellow and rarely spent extra time with the student who said he did not get it. Matt said he had made two appointments with the teacher for after-class help, but both times the teacher did not show up. We told Matt that whatever the outcome, if he had given it his best shot, then that would be all we could ask of him.

He also said that earlier that afternoon, he had taken a math classmate on a flight for her birthday. That sounded weird, so we asked him to tell us more. He said her name was Tricia and she was in his math class, and a few times they went to the same study group. Matt said Tricia was interested in learning to fly, but before she signed up for lessons, she wanted a flight in a small plane. August eighteenth was Tricia's twenty-sixth birthday, and Matt gave her a wonderful present when he took her on a flight. He told us this story with a twinkle in his eye and a grin on his face. I knew something was going on, but kept quiet.

We continued on our journey through the Caribbean, and it would be just our luck—Hurricane Debbie was headed straight toward us. We waited a day or two, and finally the captain of the ship announced he had made a decision. We would not turn back to Florida, but we would change course and visit other islands. You should have heard the grumbling. People were angry that we were going to Ocho Rios, Jamaica, when they did not pay for that! We had a wonderful time together, and we enjoyed every moment of our cruise. When we docked back at Fort Lauderdale, we said goodbye to

Matt, who had his five-hour drive to Daytona Beach and a farewell to Siobhan, who was flying to New York, and the four of us flew back to Los Angeles.

We had no idea when we would see Matt again, but we were sure something would turn up and one of us would be visiting the other.

Matt called and told us that Tricia had decided to sign up for flight lessons, so Matt now had two students. He also told us that he liked Tricia a lot. She was very smart, and he had fun with her because she liked to tease and had a dry sense of humor. He said maybe we would get the chance to meet her sometime soon. We agreed that would be nice.

Around Thanksgiving, Matt surprised us by asking if he could come home for the holiday since this year he had a more flexible schedule. We said of course, we were excited to see him, and he added, "Can I bring Tricia?"

I think Matt and Tricia had been dating since summer, and they were probably girlfriend and boyfriend by now, so, you know, we were very anxious to meet her.

On the Tuesday before Thanksgiving, Tricia had a work flight to LAX, so I would pick her up, and later in the evening, Matt would arrive and we would drive back to the airport to get him.

I arrived at the airport early, parked my car, and walked to the gate to wait for Tricia. Those were the days when one was allowed to do that without going through any kind of security. I saw Tricia's flight taxiing to the ramp and was very excited to see her. I had to wait for all the passengers to deplane and probably for the flight attendants to put all their supplies away and complete their paperwork.

Finally two flight attendants walked off wheeling their suitcases behind them, but they paid no attention to me, so I knew Tricia was still on her way. Another flight attendant got off, but she was not Tricia either. Eventually the fourth flight attendant came walking toward me, and I knew I was looking at Tricia. She was exactly as Matt had described her—tall and lanky, big blue eyes, a wide smile, and a thick Southern accent.

Her brunette ponytail was swinging as she came up to me, and when she and I hugged, I could feel her strength. She was so happy to meet me, she said, because Matt was very important to her and she wanted to meet his family.

On the drive home to Tarzana, she called her mother, Wanda, to tell her she had arrived safely and was in the car with me. We stopped at my favorite Mexican restaurant for lunch, and over chicken tacos, we got to know each other a little better. Tricia told me about her family and her home where she grew up in Tallahassee and had attended Florida State University for two years.

At home, I took her to the room where she would stay and then we went outside to sit by the pool for a while. As soon as the rest of my family came home, we would battle the traffic on the 405 and drive back to the airport. I introduced Tricia to Jeremy, Leah, and Shayna, and it was interesting to see their reactions. I think the girls were eyeing up each other. Typical girl stuff, as my husband would say.

Tricia was so excited on the ride to greet Matt. She talked about him the entire ride, and it seemed like the airport came up on us very quickly. At the gate we waited for Matt for a few minutes and then we saw him, but I saw the confusion on his face. Which one of us should he greet first? I took a step backward so Tricia was ahead of me and he would see her first. After hugs and kisses for her, it was my turn.

Matt seemed to be very happy and was glad he had found Tricia after the fiasco with Carol earlier that year.

We had dinner that evening, and I served Matt's very favorite Armenian chicken with rice pilaf, hummus, and tabbouleh. Of course, this was all wrapped up in pita bread. I told the kids that I had invited friends to the house the next evening for dessert and coffee. They liked the idea, so I went ahead and found all my mother's recipes for pumpkin and pecan pie, fruit cake, chocolate cookies and brownies, and I started making a mess in the kitchen.

Everyone was very gracious and enjoyed meeting Tricia. They also complimented me on my expertise with the delectables. We had a wonderful fun-filled evening, but the morning of Thanksgiving, Matt would get up early and take Tricia to the airport for her return flight to Orlando.

Our family ate our traditional Thanksgiving meal, quickly stacked the dishes in the dishwasher, and then went to the Great Western Forum for an LA Kings hockey game. I no longer remember who we played, and I am sure we lost the game, but, we loved it, nonetheless.

Matt and Tricia continued with their relationship for the next few months, and he told us they had gone to a New Year's Eve party and then came back to his apartment to smoke a cigar on the patio.

"A cigar?" I asked.

"Yes," he said, "a cigar. Tricia smokes cigars."

Well, I thought, *live and learn.*

Matt decided to come to visit for President's weekend, but before he did, there was a hurdle we had to cross. He asked for our advice.

Matt had started to work for a fixed base operation flight school when he moved to Daytona Beach. Julius and Tricia were his only two students. The operation was owned and run by a guy name Jim and his MEII (multi engine instrument instructor) girlfriend. Jim felt a private pilot student only needed forty hours of combined flight time and ground school instruction. At forty hours, he or she should have a private pilot's license. Matt said every student was different, and he had no problem giving his students extra time. Jim made it clear that if Matt went over the forty hours, he would not be paid. He then went to Canada to visit his family, and Matt worked the dispatch operation for the week and gave his two students their lessons in the early evening. When Jim returned, he refused to pay Matt for the forty hours he had worked, and Matt had no idea what to do. We were surprised at the dishonesty, and we advised Matt to talk to the guy and find out what he was thinking. The guy said he objected to Matt giving his students so much ground time, and he and Matt mutually agreed that Matt would no longer work there. Matt said he walked away with his dignity and felt good about the time he spent with his students.

Matt landed a job at Phil Air the next week. Julius wanted to continue taking lessons with Matt, so he followed him to Phil Air. Tricia did not. She said, "Jim didn't screw me, so why should I have to go somewhere else for my lessons?" Matt was very hurt and felt that she was disloyal. He would have followed his loved one to the moon, but he found out that she did not have the same opinion. They must have talked it over because the next thing we heard, Tricia was taking lessons with Matt.

Shortly after that incident, Tricia called me and said, "Hey, Mom Cole, guess what? I just took my first solo flight! Matt was waiting for me when I landed, and he ran over to congratulate me!"

I was very happy for her, and she said Matt followed the pilots' tradition of cutting off the back of the shirt of the guy who just soloed. She said her mother photographed Matt cutting her shirt. I have that picture.

The kids came to visit us once again for President's weekend. Matt now had about five students at Phil Air, but no one would be flying that particular weekend because of the Daytona Beach NASCAR race. Supposedly, part of the airport and runway was used for parking for spectators. We spent a wonderful weekend with Matt and Tricia, but on Monday morning we heard about an accident at the Speedway. Dale Earnhart's car crashed, and he died at the scene. We were shocked to hear this, even though, at this point, we were not avid NASCAR fans. Before they left, Tricia asked if maybe we could come to visit in Daytona Beach because she and Matt were moving into a new two-bedroom apartment together and they wanted to share this with us. I said maybe we could come when Shayna had her spring break. Matt and Jeremy would be meeting in Steamboat Springs, Colorado, to ski the first week of March.

In retrospect, I wish I could have worked on turning back the clock, or maybe checking my crystal ball to see what was coming.

As I said goodbye to Matt and Tricia as they left for Orlando, little did I know that I would never see my son like he was again. I would never see his two functional hands again or see his handsome face without scars. Very soon I would experience a heartache so painful that I never thought I would be able to laugh or smile again. At that point, I had no idea that life could be so unfair, but I was in for a very big surprise.

CHAPTER
SIX

On the first Monday in May, Bruce asked if I wanted to see the beautiful tissue that had formed on Matt's hands while they had laid buried in his groin. Bruce lifted up the blanket, and I took a look. I almost screamed. I had never seen anything so grotesque. I really had no idea what I was looking at. Prior to this surgery, Matt's hands were charred black, and his fingertips were curling up. Now I saw some sort of gray tissue covering a small portion of his hands that was protruding from the slits. Bruce told me that in the morning the hand surgeon would take Matt to the operating room and remove his hands from the flaps. He would then clean up the hands and make a quick evaluation about what would come next. In the evening, Bruce brought me the consent form, and I read every word before I signed it. I was so worried that I would miss something or misunderstand what the surgeon was about to do.

As with every surgery, I arrived early in the morning so I could stand by Matt for a few moments and put my hand on his chest so I could feel his rhythmic breathing.

I watched as Matt was wheeled down the hall to the operating room, and I was so nervous and frightened. I sat in the waiting room by myself for what seemed like hours. I held on to my book, but I read nothing. I was not able to concentrate, and my mind kept wandering.

Finally the doctor came, and he did not look happy. He told me that even though new tissue had grown on Matt's hands, it was basically useless. The blood supply was compromised, and it was difficult to find a pulse in Matt's hands. If there was no blood supply, the hands would not be able to regenerate anything new.

The doctor also said he cleaned up the new tissue on Matt's hand, but had to amputate Matt's thumb and pinkie finger on his right hand. I was hysterical and immediately called Jeremy. I have no recollection what I might have told Jeremy, and I probably got the entire story wrong.

Things were not going well, and I could not fathom what else could possibly go wrong. I felt helpless and wished I could do something for Matt. I wanted to lend a hand as Matt was wheeled back into his room, so I busied myself with the baby blanket that was covering his head.

The nurses always bundled Matt in blankets when he would return from surgery because for some reason, his body temperature would fall and it took effort to keep him warm. His head would also be wrapped in a soft baby blanket. I was attempting to pull the blanket a little tighter when something dropped into my right hand. To my complete and utter horror, it was Matt's left ear. I stood still and stared at the charred ear in my hand, and suddenly the ear was whisked from my grasp. Bruce had seen it and quickly grabbed the ear. I can feel his hands on my shoulders leading me out of the room. Once again I was unable to speak, and I thought I might be sick.

Bruce said it was okay. Everything was all right. His magic words to me were, "Mom Cole, it's fixable. Don't worry. This can be fixed."

I wondered how much more we would have to fix. I did not sleep that night because I had nightmares about my child's ear falling into my hand. I know some people might say it was just an ear, but I felt that I was losing Matt little by little. And his body was falling apart a small amount every day.

May was turning into a glorious month, but my stomach hurt most of the time. I was not eating, and I was still losing weight.

On the first Friday of May, I was buzzed into the burn unit, and as I passed the nurses' station, Miss Joyce told me I was in for a big surprise today.

She said, "I think you'll like this."

Sue Mary and Jody held up their hands and told me to wait while they finished a chore in Matt's room. I heard them talking, but I assumed they were speaking to each other.

Finally Sue Mary said, "Come on in, Gerry. Matt's awake and waiting for you!"

What did she say?

I walked in slowly, and to my delight, Matt was sitting in a wheelchair and looking at me! Oh, how I cried again: I had no idea one five-foot-two-inch person could squeeze out so many tears! Miss Joyce was behind me and was laughing. Sue Mary and Jody were laughing.

Matt was unable to speak because of his tracheostomy tube, but he mouthed to me, "Hi, Mom."

Those two little words were like a symphony to my ears. I was so excited, but now did not know what to say to Matt. I had no idea how much he knew or remembered about the accident, and I was afraid I would upset him. Sue Mary told me she had discussed with him where he was and what had happened to him, and she said he nodded yes and no to her when she asked if he remembered the crash.

Matt continued to stare at me and then mouthed, "My ass hurts!"

I had no idea that he had a huge decubitus bed sore on his coccyx, his tailbone, and it was very painful.

Then he said to me, "I miss you."

I said he had no idea how much I had missed him, but I was there with him and we would get through this. He nodded okay and said that would be good.

A few hours later, Tricia walked through the door and shocked Matt. He thought she had left him after the accident. She said she was not going anywhere. I stood back and cried again, wondering if I would ever stop crying and sniffling.

Matt tired very easily, and his decubitus was hurting, so he was put back to bed and promptly fell asleep. Tricia and I watched him sleep for a while and then we went out for dinner. For the first time in two months, I realized my stomach was not hurting and I was hungry. I ate an entire chicken breast and ate every morsel of my vegetables. It was the first full meal I had eaten since mid-March.

Tricia went back to work, and once again I was alone with Matt. He continued to sleep on and off, and on Friday of that week he was in his wheelchair again. He continued to complain about his decubitus. By now we had met Jeff and Eddie, the physical therapist and occupational therapist who came every day to exercise Matt's legs.

While he was sitting in his chair looking around, a visitor walked into his room. Matt stretched to a more straight-up position, his eyes got really big, he had a smile on his face, and he screamed, "Leah!"

His sister had just walked through the door. When she saw him, she dropped the package she was carrying and ran toward him. She hugged him so ferociously I thought they would both fall over. I had no idea how Matt was able to get sound out, but from that point, he started to talk to us, and did he ever talk.

This weekend that Leah visited was Mother's Day, so this was an especially wonderful day for me. I had my oldest daughter with me, plus Matt was speaking. He told me he had no time to buy me a present, so he hoped I would not be too upset. I knew immediately I was seeing his sense of humor coming out, and I loved every snide remark he shot in my direction.

Leah took me out for brunch, and Matt's friend Paddy Hyndman came to visit so he joined us. When we returned to the burn unit, Matt was sound asleep and Sue Mary told us that Matt was now off morphine and Ativan completely, so he would continue to lapse into sleep and would have some lucid moments. I was so disappointed, but I took whatever I could.

That evening Paddy left for Daytona Beach, and Leah flew back to Los Angeles. Tricia returned from her workweek, so we would be alone for the next few days.

We heard a lot of noise coming from the hallway, so we looked out to see what was happening. Yard Dog was in charge of Matt that evening, and he told us to stay put in the room. He then walked out and closed the door. Tricia wondered why we were left alone with Matt since up until that point, a nurse was busy in the room constantly. I had a theory that Matt was stable and on the way to recovery and did not require constant watching.

Yard Dog was gone for over an hour, and when he returned, he told us that upon checking, Matt was stable and sleeping comfortably. Unfortunately, another patient had been brought in from Jacksonville, Florida, and he was burned over 60 percent of his body. He was forty-seven years old, had hypertension and diabetes, and his chances for survival were bleak. His mother and five older sisters were waiting outside the unit, and their last name was Palmer. Yard Dog told us that it looked like someone was trying to murder Mr. Palmer since a lighted torch was thrown into his house, ignited the roof, and Mr. Palmer slept while his house burned down. When he awoke, he was on fire, and he ran outside. I never heard what happened, who put out the flames, or how he ended up in Gainesville. I just know that his mother had a huge impact on my life. I will never forget her or what she taught me.

She and I were two women from totally different backgrounds, but we had so much in common. It never mattered that she was in her eighties and I was in my fifties, or that she was black and I was white, or certainly not that she was Baptist and I Jewish. The common denominator was our relationship with our sons. Everything was about our sons and their well-being.

Mrs. Palmer and I would sit together in the waiting room while our boys were in surgery, and quite often we would go to the cafeteria for a cup of tea. She loved tea, but the cafeteria did not have green tea, which was her favorite, so she started to bring her own bags to share with me. Over steaming mugs, we learned about each other's sons and families and our hopes and wishes for our children. We both shared the same fear, losing our child. I remember having one particularly gut-wrenching conversation with her; after this life-altering event, how do we pick up the pieces? Mrs. Palmer said we would continue on just as before because first and foremost, our boys needed their mothers, and that is what we were—mothers in pain, but mothers, nonetheless—and she said we would continue to act the way Matt and Whit expected us to.

She then surprised me by saying, "Let's go upstairs and visit the boys."

When we arrived in the unit, we put on our smocks and walked to Whit's room. I was holding Mrs. Palmer's hand, and I heard her quickly say, "I can do this." And once again, "Whit, I can do this."

I could barely walk into the room with her. I smelled burned flesh again, and I saw a thin person being perfectly still in the bed. Mr. Palmer had more pumps than Matt did, and he was connected to a Swan-Ganz heart catheter for some sort of cardiac problem, something Matt never had.

Then we walked the short distance to Matt's room. We had to wash our hands and put on clean smocks and gloves. When Mrs. Palmer grasped my hand. I could feel how strong she was despite her frail stature.

She looked at Matt, who was sleeping so peacefully, took a deep breath and said, "I can feel the goodness in this room. Can you feel it?"

I honestly had no idea what she was talking about, so I merely nodded.

She said, "The Lord doesn't want Matt yet, so he'll have to work hard to recover. He has a good heart and is needed to do something very important."

Once again I dumbly nodded and wondered where she would come up with such a theory. I decided she was trying to make me feel better, which she did, but I was sorry I lacked the panache to comfort her.

The days wore on in May, and Matt continued to drift in and out of sleep. He was still on morphine and Ativan, but was steadily being weaned.

One evening Yard Dog rolled in a leather lounge chair for me to sit in and hopefully be more comfortable. I would sit in the chair and read or write in my journal. Or I would just sit and listen to Matt breathe. That was such a comforting sound—no ventilator, no pumps beeping, just normal breathing.

One night it was starting to get dark. Matt was sleeping, or so I thought, but I heard him whisper, "Mom, are you here?"

I said, "I'm sitting right here."

He said, "Come closer."

I stood up and went to his bedside.

He said, "Mom, too low, too slow. Be careful!"

Now what the heck did that mean? I had no chance to ask Matt because he had immediately fallen asleep.

For the next four nights, he kept saying, "Too low, too slow. Be careful."

On the sixth night I got it.

He said, "We're too low and we're going too slow. Watch out for the trees!"

I realized he was dreaming or going over the moments before the plane crashed. Witnesses had used those exact words when explaining what they saw. The plane was too low, was going too slow, and the right wing was clipping trees. I started to have nightmares about a flaming airplane chasing me, and I was having a difficult time outrunning the plane. I would always hide under a bridge of some sort, and the plane would keep on going.

One evening Yard Dog dragged me out from under the lounge chair. I guess that had been the bridge in my dream. We laughed about my behavior and were grateful I had no back problems because how would I ever get out from under that chair if I had pain?

On the third Friday of May, I decided I had to find a synagogue, so Sumner at the nurses' station went online and found the closest temple for me to attend Sabbath evening services.

Matt was whispering his concern for me because a huge rainstorm had come into Gainesville, and Matt said since I was not familiar with the city, he was worried about flooding. I left him with Tricia and went to services anyway.

The temple was very modest, and we sat on folding chairs. The rabbi called me up to the bema, and I lighted the Sabbath candles, something traditionally done by the mother as she serves the Sabbath eve meal. As I lit the candles and chanted the Hebrew prayer, I had a flash of doing this once before the night preceding Matt's Bar Mitzvah. I could even remember the dress I was wearing and seeing

Matt, Jeremy, Leah, Shayna, my mother, and Jeremy's mom and dad watching me from the front row pews.

As I continued to light those two Sabbath candles, I was brought back to reality by the rabbi telling the congregation to turn to page so and so in their prayer books for the next prayer.

I stayed for the Oneg Shabbat, hosted by the family of tomorrow morning's Bar Mitzvah boy. The Oneg Shabbat is a snack served after Friday evening services and consists of assorted cookies, coffee, tea, and punch for the kids. It is usually hosted by the family of the boy or girl who will have his or her Bar or Bat Mitzvah in the morning. I met some of the people there and received hugs and good wishes from all the people I spoke to. I left the temple with a feeling of strength and contentment. I was anxious to return to the unit to see Matt and Tricia. When I returned, I was in for a big surprise. Matt was awake and was hallucinating—big time. Bruce said it was very normal for patients to behave like this when they are coming off morphine. I was frightened anyway.

Matt was whispering, as usual, and he was very funny. He asked me to kindly remove the rabbits that were sitting on his arms. I asked him what rabbits he was talking about, and he lost his patience with me.

He said, "Are you blind, Mom? The white rabbits that are sitting on my arms!"

His arms and hands were wrapped in gauze and bandages, and, yes, they were white, but to me they did not look like rabbits. To hear the inflection in Matt's voice was very comical, but I was so concerned. Even though Matt had always had a great sense of humor, he was not usually silly.

The next morning, I questioned the doctor and asked him how one responds to hallucinations. His advice was not wonderful.

He said, "You know your son better than anyone, so do what you think will work."

Terrific.

Monday morning rolled around bringing sunshine and warmth, and I was back in the burn unit. I had just arrived when Sue Mary told me a visitor was looking for me. I could not imagine who that might be. To my surprise, one of the ladies from the temple had shown up with a pot roast. She must have set her alarm clock for five o'clock that morning to prepare the meal for us. I could not believe it. Later I shared the pot roast with everyone, and we enjoyed the scrumptious treat. How could I ever thank her? After Matt's nap, Nurse Pablo came into the room carrying the biggest balloon bouquet I had ever seen.

Matt said, "Who sent that? Mom, read the card."

It was a gift from all the folks I had met at services the previous Friday. It was signed by the Bernsteins, Levines, Golds, Cokers, and Rosenbergs.

The card said, "To Matt... We met your Mom Friday and hope you know our congregation is cheering for you and praying for a speedy recovery."

To my surprise, Matt started to cry and said, "But I don't know these people."

I said it did not matter. Hearing about him made everyone want to send him good wishes. He said okay and promptly fell asleep.

Tricia and I sat in Matt's room quietly speaking when she said she had to make a few phone calls. I said that was fine with me, so I just sat in the corner in my comfortable lounge chair and wrote in my journal. I heard Tricia call her friend Lisa and ask her to be the maid of honor at her wedding. Then she called her friend Nilsa and asked her to be the maid of honor at her wedding. Finally she called her friend Julie and asked her to be the maid of honor at her wedding. Tricia always spoke loudly on her cell phone, so even if I were totally deaf, I would probably hear what she was saying. I found myself wondering what was happening. I did not want to meddle, but I assumed if she were planning a wedding, it would be to my son, so did that mean I had the right to know her plans? I decided to go for it I asked her what was happening. She said she and Matt had discussed marriage, and as soon as he was better, they would start planning for their future together. I thought this was a bit premature given Matt's situation, but if planning a wedding kept her going, who was I to criticize? But these maids of honor? How did that work?

I continued to visit with Mrs. Palmer, whose son was still fighting for his life. I would bring her tea up to the unit, and Tricia and I would always share our pizza with her when we had it delivered. One night Bruce told us that Mr. Palmer had gone into renal failure and may not make it through the night. I was very upset as I left that evening for my apartment. I slept poorly and kept thinking about my dear friend.

The next morning as I rounded the corner to the burn unit, I saw Mrs. Palmer sitting on the chair. I was so glad to see her. That meant Whit had made it through the night. I bugged her and told her I had prayed for her and Whit all night.

She said, "Honey child, that's what I need."

She added, "But you know my precious Whit is not doing well."

I said I had heard, but we would all hope for the best and continue to pray for him. Whit's sisters came through the doors, and we all gathered and hugged for a few minutes. Their family was allowed in, but I had to wait for Matt to finish his bath. When I went in, Sue Mary told me that Matt had enjoyed his bath time. Matt was awake, and when I looked at him, he rolled his eyes at me. I learned that bath time was no fun for the burn survivor who would be wheeled into "the tank," where he would be scrubbed clean. I'm told it hurt tremendously. After that, Matt's legs would be slathered with Silvadene and wrapped with Xeroform and gauze. His leg skin had been used as donor sites, creating a second-degree burn, and they were having a hard time healing.

Matt said to me out of earshot of everyone, "They're gonna kill me!"

I tried not to smile because, in fact, Matt was getting the best medical care available, and Dr. Mozingo and his staff had first saved his life. But Matt still had some confusion and still came out with some zingers that made everyone laugh.

Later that day we heard that Mr. Palmer was in pulmonary failure and had ARDS. He was on the ventilator and dialysis but still was not doing well and was in his room when he died.

I found Mrs. Palmer in the hallway and hugged her again. I told her how sorry I was for her loss and I would pray for her.

She said to me, "My journey with my son has come to an end, but yours is just beginning. Matt will need you more than ever now. Don't let him down. Show him the strength I've seen in you, and his journey will be easier. Be firm with him as he recovers, but be fair. Make sure he knows how much you love him. Tell him every day. Remind him every day and never let him forget that fact."

I kissed her goodbye and watched her walk down the hall with her daughters. I was sad to know I would never see her again but happy to know our paths had crossed despite the disastrous circumstances. Later that day I learned that the name Palmer was an alias because of the suspicious way Mr. Palmer had been burned. I could not believe it. I never even knew such a great lady's real name.

CHAPTER
SEVEN

"Who is that chick?" asked Matt, "and why is she staring at me?"

Tricia and I looked around but thought we were the only chicks in the room.

Matt was staring at his balloon bouquet that was in the corner of his room. In the middle of the group was a bright yellow Mylar balloon with a smiley face.

I decided to play along with him, so I walked over and pointed to the smiley face and said, "This girl?"

He said, "Yes. Ask her if she has a problem. She keeps looking at me."

I said, "She probably appreciates a handsome guy when she sees one!"

Without missing a beat, he said, "Well, thank goodness she's Jewish!"

Oh, how we laughed at that one.

Around this same time, Bruce told us that he thought very shortly Matt would ask for a mirror so he could see his face. I said Matt had never been a very vain young man, so I thought he would not ask to look at himself. Boy, was I wrong.

On a quiet afternoon about three days later, Matt said to me, "Mom, has my face been rearranged?"

My heart skipped a beat as I said there was no rearrangement. Just burns.

To my surprise, he said, "Do you have a mirror in your purse?"

Luckily I did not, but he said to find Bruce and get a mirror.

I walked out to the hallway and said to Bruce, "I need your help!"

He said, "Matt wants a mirror, right?"

I said, "Yes."

So Bruce found a hand mirror in a drawer, and we walked into the room together. Bruce asked me if he should hold the mirror up for Matt, but I said I would do it. When I held the mirror up for Matt and he looked at his face, he started to cry. For once, I held it together and did not turn into the emotional wimp that I thought I had become, but inside my heart was breaking for Matt.

He said to me, "Boy, I'm a mess, aren't I?"

I said, "Remember your face was burned and it is still healing... the healing process will go on for quite some time."

Matt then said, "Where are my ears?"

I said, "They had been burned very badly, and they sloughed off." I said, "Just know we can get prosthetic ears made for you."

He said, "Are you sure?"

I said, "Of course. A lot of your concerns and worries can be fixed." I said, "But let's take one day at a time and get to the point where we can get you out of the burn unit and head for home."

He said, "That's a deal, Mom."

I put the mirror down and gave it back to Bruce.

I said thank you to him, and he said, "I didn't do anything. You and Matt handled it by yourselves."

I believe at that point, Bruce had given me a true gift—the knowledge and self-confidence I needed to help Matt. Up until that point, I had been faltering, and I was very unsure of myself. I was afraid to say anything to Matt because I was so afraid of hurting or upsetting him, but I realized that Matt was going to be very open to discussions about the accident and about what happened to him.

I had said to Bruce earlier on that I was so worried about Matt's outcome because I mistakenly thought this accident and injury had happened to my weakest child. I sure did make a huge error on that one. I equated my daughters' strong opinions as strength and Matt's quiet, humble demeanor as weakness. I learned a valuable lesson because I could see that Matt exhibited a great amount of patience and quiet self-confidence. I spent hours sitting in my comfortable lounge chair in Matt's room. I was now able to focus on my book, so I read a lot and wrote in my journal. Matt would sleep a lot, and he was often confused.

One afternoon he said to me, "Hey, Mom, are you hungry?"

I said, "No, I'm fine."

He said, "Are these clowns ever gonna feed me here?"

He was still on his feeding tubes and had no food yet. He said he was starving. I told Sue Mary that Matt was hungry, and she said she thought it would only be a few days more and Dr. Mozingo would write the order for food. Matt said he would start the countdown.

That evening, he was extremely confused and was hallucinating. He was lying on his special air mattress that would move him from side to side to alleviate the pain in his decubitus. Matt thought he was on an airplane.

When Rhonda, the night nurse, walked in, he yelled at her, "Take your seat. We're on our way to Tokyo, and I don't want to keep the passengers waiting!"

I had no idea where this came from, but I think the motor on his bed reminded him of the din of an airplane engine.

She murmured, "Yes, Captain!" and walked out with a smile.

When she walked in a little later, he said, "Didn't you feel that turbulence? Take your seat!"

Poor Rhonda. She was such a good sport. She told me it was rewarding to hear him yelling at her even though he was confused.

A few minutes later, he said to me, "Mom, do you have any food in your purse? A sandwich? Anything? I'm starving!"

He screamed once more at Rhonda, "What's a guy have to do around here to get a lunch platter?"

She said she would look to see what she could find for him. She returned with a Styrofoam cup filled with ice chips that had been drizzled with a small amount of root beer.

Matt said to Rhonda, "'You disappoint me. I was hoping for some sushi."

The next morning Sue Mary told me that Matt would now be allowed food, but he had to take it easy. He was down to 105, so he had lost about thirteen pounds. Matt said he wanted McDonald's, but I offered him Wendy's since that was available in the hospital cafeteria.

When I offered him his Coke, he drank it down very quickly. Then he started to cry. He said nothing had ever tasted so good. As I was holding his hamburger for him, he took small bites and seemed to savor every morsel that he was chewing.

He then stopped eating, looked at me, and very seriously said, "Mom, I'm awfully glad to be here!"

I couldn't resist. No one had said anything to me about not touching Matt or the risk of infection for a long time, so I took Matt in my arms and held him as close as I could. I told him over and over how much I loved him and how I thanked God every day for not taking him away from me.

Matt was suddenly frightened about his future. He was worried about not being able to take care of himself. And he was aghast when I gave him lunch that he was unable to feed himself. I told him to stay focused on recovering and his family would help him any way we could. I also told him over and over that gratefully he did not suffer a head injury and he had a good brain. He could accomplish anything in life that he wanted, with or without hands.

On the last Saturday of May, Matt's good friend Yoav called on my cell phone. He had called every Saturday since Matt had been admitted to the hospital. Our conversations were always the same.

"Hi, Gerry," Yoav would say. "Is Matt awake?"

"Not yet," I would say.

"Well, if he wakes up, tell him I'm thinking about him."

"Okay," I would say.

But the end of May was different, Matt was awake, so when my phone rang, I remarked that it must be Yoav.

"Get the phone quickly," Matt said.

So when Yoav asked his usual "Is Matt awake?"

I said, "Yes, do you want to speak to him?"

There was silence. I think Yoav was surprised to hear that response. I explained to Yoav that Matt could not speak above a whisper and I would have to hold the phone for him. Matt was very anxious to speak to his friend, but when I put the phone to his ear, his "Hi, man" came out as a squeak more than a voice. I held the phone while Yoav explained everything that had been happening in Los Angeles and what friends had sent their regards. Matt mostly sniffled, and I saw a few tears roll down his cheeks.

I was always very touched that Yoav never gave up. His phone calls meant a lot to Matt and to me, and we found ourselves waiting for the Saturday afternoon phone calls from him.

June was just around the corner, and Shayna was thinking about her high school graduation.

I told Matt I was going home for a few days to attend the ceremony and to take Shayna out to celebrate, and he said, "I want to go, too. I should be there. I'm Shayna's big bro. I should be at her graduation."

I explained to him that we all understood that he was unable to attend, and even though Shayna wanted him there, she knew why he would not be. And besides, I would be back in a few days. Tricia had a few days off so she would stay with him.

I was traveling on one of Tricia's Delta Airlines buddy passes, and I was lucky enough to get on the first flight out of Gainesville and on an immediate flight out of Atlanta. I arrived at LAX mid-morning and was met at the airport by my friend Sona Rosenberg. We had a nice time together and had lunch and then we went back to my house. When I walked through the door, I was greeted by my friend and housekeeper, Maria. She hugged me and cried and wanted to know all about Matt. I told her I was just here for Shayna's graduation and would be going back to Gainesville as soon as possible. But she was glad to see me anyway.

The morning of Shayna's graduation, we awoke to "June gloom," the typical overcast mornings that we would experience during June in Southern California. I sat down at the kitchen table with my coffee, and Shayna joined me before she left for graduation rehearsal and to pick up her cap and gown. She seemed very sad and quiet. I thought she would be excited to be finished with high school, but instead she came across as depressed.

I asked her what was wrong, and she burst into tears.

"How can I go to graduation without Matt?" she asked.

I certainly could feel her pain, but I explained Matt was cheering for her from his hospital bed. After I finished saying that, the phone rang. Shayna answered it, and even though she had tears in her eyes, her face lit up like a Christmas tree. It was her brother whistling Elgar's Pomp and Circumstance for her. He said he was just getting her ready for the ceremony. Shayna was delighted, and the remainder of the day passed uneventfully.

In the evening, we arrived at the school and encountered the usual San Fernando Valley chaos. With over seven hundred graduates and all their relatives, there was a lot of traffic. We found our way to the football field and climbed onto the bleachers. This year the ceremony was being held at eight o'clock rather than the traditional six o'clock because the principal's daughter was graduating from another high school at six o'clock. Since there was a conflict, the parents agreed to change the time to eight o'clock.

The ceremony went on endlessly. There were about seven hundred and fifty graduates, and with all the speeches, awards, and band's musical selections, it was dark when the exercises ended. Suddenly all the lights on the field went out. It was pitch black, and you could not see two inches in front of you. All at once, the first firework flew up into the sky, and the audience roared. The fireworks display was gorgeous, but no one expected it. The principal had arranged this surprise for the graduates to thank everyone for accommodating her and allowing her to go to her child's graduation. What an exciting evening, but when the lights went on, I could see that Leah had been crying. I knew what she had been thinking. How Matt would have enjoyed this.

I had decided to return to Gainesville on Monday morning, but on Sunday morning, we received a phone call from Tricia. She was very excited and said she had some news for us. Matt had proposed to her! She was very excited and said all the nurses were congratulating her and wishing her well. And most of them wanted to be invited to the wedding.

My trip back to Gainesville was a fiasco. Even though I appreciated the buddy pass from Tricia and the price was right, it was a tough way to travel. First, I had difficulty getting out of LAX and finally got onto the third flight to Atlanta. Once there, I was unable to get onto anything flying to Gainesville. I guess everyone was going there for some reason. I ended up sitting in the Atlanta airport for nineteen hours. I was very agitated and probably should have rented a car and driven to Gainesville. I never arrived until Tuesday morning.

I drove straight to the hospital and found Matt to be very crabby. When I said good morning to him, he gave me a very sour "hi."

Sue Mary said, "Guess what? It's moving day!"

I said, "Who's moving?"

She said, "Matt is going to rehab!"

I had no idea what was going on, and I wondered where rehab was. Sue Mary said the ambulance would be coming shortly and I could ride with him.

A few minutes later, a guy named Gary came to find Matt, and he helped Sue Mary wheel Matt on his gurney down to the waiting ambulance.

Matt was very upset and was yelling at me, "How could you let them do this to me?"

Sue Mary and I both explained to him that I had no control over this situation and that Dr. Mozingo decided Matt was ready for rehab. We walked out of the burn unit with Matt in a huff. This was not how I had envisioned our exit, but it had turned out that way because of Matt's attitude. After we loaded Matt onto the ambulance, Sue Mary hugged me and I climbed up the stairs and sat down next to Matt, who was now pouting and not speaking to me. At this point, I had no idea how frightened he was. I decided to make conversation.

I said, "You must be apprehensive about going to rehab because I'm scared too. Let's consider this to be a new adventure where we'll learn new things."

He said, "I can't even walk. How can I go to rehab?"

I explained that I thought that was the reason for rehab—to get him on his feet again, literally.

Matt was extremely frail, but I was told he was holding steady at a thirteen-pound weight loss. He had severe foot drop from lying on his back for three months, and his legs were not strong enough to bold him up.

The director of the rehab center told us where to go, so I helped Matt settle into his new room. I tacked his Acura NSX poster on the bulletin board and set up photos of all of us on the table.

We immediately met a guy named Karl, who introduced himself to us as Matt's physical therapist. Karl came with his rule book, and Matt would be expected in the gym in about fifteen minutes.

Matt said, "Mom, you've just put me in boot camp!"

I said it was about time he got to work to recover quicker because I had had enough of Florida. I could feel the Santa Ana winds of Southern California, and I wanted to go home.

As we sat and waited for Karl to come back and take Matt to the gym, Jacquie walked in. She was the most ebullient, fun-loving young lady I had ever met. She had Matt in stitches. All through Matt's stay in rehab, she would tease him unmercifully, and he loved to banter with her.

Karl showed me how to put Matt in a sitting position and then how to transfer him to the wheelchair. Matt was nothing but skin and bones in my hands, and I easily transferred him to the wheelchair.

That first day in rehab felt like I was on an emotional roller coaster. On the one hand, I knew Matt had recovered to the point where the rehabilitation would start, and that was good. On the other hand, Matt was so weak and so frail and was unable to walk. He would be given morphine before his physical therapy session, but that made him sleepy, and he would negotiate with Karl. Matt would want to take a nap, and Karl said, "No way," it was time to work.

The first few days in rehab, Matt was wheeled to the gym in his chair, but on the fourth day, Karl said, "Let's take a walk to the gym!"

Matt said, "Are you kidding?"

Karl said, "I never kid about such things. Let's go!"

Karl had taught Matt to swing his legs off the bed, firmly plant both feet on the floor, and stand up. Luckily, Matt never complained of dizziness or light-headedness. He was just weak, and it was difficult to hoist his body to a standing position. Sometimes he had to try two or three times.

On this day, however, he was able to stand up on his first try. We walked very slowly down the hall with Karl next to Matt, Tricia in front of him, and me behind Matt with the wheelchair; just in case. When we approached the nurses' station, everyone started to cheer and applaud for Matt. Even the patients who were milling about were excited for him. Suddenly Matt started to run. He was now so motivated and wanted to do everything he could. Karl had to tell him to slow down.

Matt continued to improve and worked very hard with Karl and all the folks in the gym. He learned how to run again and how to climb stairs. I have a photo of Matt with Karl, and it is noticeable that Matt's neck is frozen into a downward position. He was developing spots that would have to be "released" to promote movement.

On the Fourth of July, Tricia decided to run a marathon in Gainesville. She was up early and left for the park. She and I decided we would meet at the rehab center when she was finished with the run. There would be a special barbeque for all the patients and their families, and we wanted to include Matt.

When Tricia returned, she was in a foul mood. She did not speak to me, nor to Matt for that matter, and when she finished reading a magazine, she tossed it into a corner and walked out of the room. I had no idea what to make of such strange behavior. We had not had a falling-out, but obviously something had happened. Matt said to pay no attention to her. He said she would get moody often and it was best to ignore her. I worried all day because I had no idea how to handle this situation and I thought it was my job to fix it,

We went to the barbeque, and Matt had hamburgers and hot dogs and his favorite baked beans. He also had an ice cream cone, but said he felt like a toddler because I had to hold the cone for him so he could eat it and it was melting faster than he could lick. We were both a mess.

When we came back to the room, it was time to exercise Matt's mouth. He hated this exercise, but we did it at least twice a day. I would put on a surgical glove and run my finger around the inside of Matt's mouth. Then we would make vowel sounds to open and close, pucker or squeeze his lips together. His lips were healing and getting very tight. We wanted to make sure he could open and close his mouth and do all the movements we take for granted. Matt understood but hated these exercises anyway. Looking back on it, I am so glad we kept them up because they helped tremendously.

Shayna was returning from the Caribbean cruise with friends, her graduation gift, and wanted to visit Matt. The cost of flights from Miami to Gainesville was astronomical, so Paddy Hyndman offered to drive me to Miami to meet Shayna's ship and bring her back to visit Matt. It was a long drive to Miami, but when Shayna saw me standing there with Paddy, she ran up to the two of us for hugs. Leah was on the same ship, but she had to get back to her job and would visit another time.

The ride back to Gainesville was long, but we finally arrived at the rehab center. Shayna was anxious to see Matt. She had not seen him since March, and she was eager to talk to him.

Paddy and I escorted her to Matt's room, and when she walked in and saw him, she ran to her brother and hugged him as tight as she could. Matt burst into tears. This upset Shayna tremendously, and she, too, started to cry. They were holding each other and crying, which I felt gave me carte blanche to join in.

Matt said to Shayna, "These are happy tears, not sad ones."

I had never heard him use those words before, so I assume the therapist that Matt saw every morning was working on dealing with emotions. Suffice it to say, Shayna was ecstatic to see Matt, and she sat on the side of the bed and held his arm.

He was very comfortable with that, and he kept looking at her and saying, "I love you, Shayna. I'm so glad you came to visit. How long can you stay?"

I could tell Shayna was upset, but was doing her best to keep it together.

Tricia and I took Shayna to Sea World in Orlando, and we went to some sort of springs. We rented tubes and a raft for me, and the movement of the springs kept us moving. The water was ice cold, but what a peaceful two hours we spent traveling those springs. I felt so calm, and I almost fell asleep on my raft. Of course I kept thinking of Matt and wondering what he was doing that afternoon. I was always anxious to get back to him because I knew how he loved having one of us around all the time. I knew, also, that he became very sad if he was left alone, and I hated that.

I took Shayna to the airport on Friday evening, but before that, Matt showed her how he could jog around the gym and run up and down the makeshift stairs and how he could do some crunches on the ball. He just had no working hands. All his exercising involved his lower body. After his gym session, we went to the kitchen for ice cream. Tricia helped Matt eat, and he loved the extra rich chocolate ice cream that we found for him in the freezer.

After Shayna left, Tricia went to work for a few days, so as usual, Matt and I were alone. Everything was going along smoothly. Our routine was therapy and gym in the morning after a shower and wound care, which took almost two hours. I would always go somewhere to pick up something for lunch for us. Matt loved the sushi from a restaurant I had found near the university, and he enjoyed the soups I would bring from the Italian restaurant that was next to the rehab center. I have a feeling those foods were not too nutritious and he did not consume enough calories, but at least he was eating. Sometimes I would dash out to Dairy Queen and return with a thick chocolate shake. Now those had plenty of calories, and Matt loved the treat.

In the afternoon, it was back to the gym for more physical therapy and more mouth exercises. By four thirty, Matt would be so tired that he would have to drag himself back to his room. I would help him onto his bed and cover him up. He would always fall asleep immediately. That was my time to go back to my apartment to prepare dinner for us. We usually ate chicken of some sort, and Matt loved it that I had dinner with him. As I said before, he hated to be alone. Consequently I was spending all my time at the hospital, but I was with Matt, he was alive, and life was good.

Tricia came home from work that Friday, and at around four in the afternoon, we were called to the nurses' station, where we were told Matt would be leaving rehab on Tuesday.

I said, "Where are we going?"

She said, "Home or anywhere you want to take him!"

Our health insurance had decided Matt had recovered as much as he could, so they were done giving him benefits. I was shocked and had no idea what to do next.

Tricia, who was standing next to me, said, "Well, we'll just have to rent an RV and drive home!"

The insurance company loved that, so we had to get out. And, oh, yes, they would give Matt an air mattress. I was wracking my brain about what to do when Dr. Mozingo called me from the hospital. I assume he had heard what was happening, so he decided to put Matt back in the hospital and start the reconstructive process. First, he would "release" Matt's neck so he could regain movement. Then he would "release" Matt's underarms so he could raise his arms. That sounded like a good idea to me, plus that would buy us a little time.

Tuesday morning, at about dawn, the ambulance came to retrieve Matt. Tricia and I dressed him in his boxer shorts with airplanes, new comfy pants, socks, and new slip-on sneakers. We were unable to get a shirt on him because his arms had no bend, so even though we heard that Dr. Mozingo wanted to see his patients dressed, we put Matt's hospital smock back on.

I drove behind the ambulance carrying Matt and Tricia, and I met them, once again, in the burn unit. Sue Mary and Jody hugged me and were glad to have Matt back on their floor again.

The next morning Matt went to surgery, and Tricia and I were back in the waiting room. There were no new burns in the unit, so things seemed really quiet. After surgery, Matt would be put back in his old room.

Dr. Mozingo came to talk to us after he completed the release of Matt's neck. He said all went well, but Matt, who had never really met Dr. Mozingo before, said to him, "I didn't know you looked so much like a broom!"

I was surprised Matt would say that, but Dr. Mozingo had a bristly mustache, and he, indeed, looked like a broom. The nurses said the doctor had a great sense of humor and had probably enjoyed Matt's comments. We also heard that Matt was concerned about his new boxers with the airplanes. They were his favorite! After the surgery, Big Mike brought me a package with all Matt's clothes neatly folded with his new shoes in a plastic bag.

We spent the next week with Matt and Jeff and Eddie, who came back now to exercise Matt's neck. The surgery seemed to be successful because when Matt sat up, his head was upright and not looking down at the floor. And he said he could move his head from side to side, but not easily.

The following week found us in the waiting room again while Dr. Mozingo worked on Matt's underarms. They were so tight that skin was taken from Matt's hip and placed under his arm, giving him more space to move.

When he returned from the operating room, I was shocked. Matt's face was bruised, his lips were swollen, his eyes were black, and there was a blob of some sort on the bridge of his nose. He looked like he had been in a fight and had lost. Dr. Mozingo told me that he had a chunk of extra skin from Matt's hip, so he had placed it on his nose.

The next few days were very difficult for Matt because his arms were raised above his head and tied to the bed. Jody would come in every now and then to tighten them. After about three days and Matt crying in agonizing pain, his arms were untied, and Jeff and Eddie came for the exercising.

Matt wanted to know everything, so I would walk around the unit with him and show him where we would be buzzed in and how we had to put on our smocks and gloves and where we had our meetings with the doctor in the conference room.

Matt was becoming very popular, and everyone was very happy to meet the guy he was before his accident. He may have been scarred, his body battered, and his hands lost, but he was still Matt. His sense of humor was still there, as evidenced by his love of a good joke. Every day Yard Dog would come to work with a new joke for Matt, and he would double over with laughter.

Steadily, my stomach had settled down, and I was dreaming of home. I was wondering how much longer we would have to stay here. Lurking around the corner was another crisis that would set us back to a point where I thought I would completely lose it. So severe would it be I thought we would never recover.

CHAPTER
EIGHT

"I feel sick," Matt said to me in the second week of August.
He said that one of the nurses had fed him scrambled eggs and toast for breakfast, and consequently he was feeling nauseous. Matt refused lunch and was restless all day. He complained all afternoon about his stomach and would not get out of bed to walk around.

When dinner came around and he was still was nauseous, I became concerned. Dr. Mozingo had ordered Compazine for his nausea, but it did not seem to be helping. Tricia and I stayed with Matt until around eleven that night. We covered him up, gave him kisses, told him we hoped he felt better in the morning, turned out the light, and started to walk out of his room.

That's when we heard the first sounds of someone vomiting. We turned on the light, and sure enough, Matt had vomited all over the floor, the bed, and himself. He was lying flat on his back, so I quickly raised the head of his bed so he would not aspirate, and Tricia rushed out to call the nurse.

We helped Rhonda change the linens, clean up Matt, and we waited for the call from the resident ordering more Compazine.

This time Matt was given a shot in his behind, and we waited until he fell asleep.

Tricia and I came home to my apartment well after midnight, and I was exhausted. I slept in my clothes that night because I was too tired to put on my pajamas, but I kept waking up because I was worrying if Matt was feeling better.

The next day we learned that Matt had been vomiting all night and was really under the weather. An IV had been put in his foot to give him fluids because he was so dehydrated. This illness, or whatever it was, kept on for five days, and Matt looked like he was wasting away. I could tell he was getting thinner, and the vomiting continued.

Nothing was coming up but stomach fluids, and Matt was looking really sick.

The IV was continued in his foot, and an NG, or nasogastric tube, was placed down his nose and into his stomach. A bucket was set behind his bed, and every few hours, the nurse would have to empty it. I was told the NG tube would not be removed until no more gastric juices emptied into that bucket. But that was not happening. I watched the nurses change that container more and more often. Matt was down to ninety-two pounds, and he was not feeling any better. If anything, he said he felt worse.

I kept calling Jeremy asking if he had any thoughts or if he had spoken to Matt's doctors.

I was becoming desperate. No one knew what was wrong or why Matt was so ill.

I thought, for the third time, Matt was dying. And I was not willing to let that happen. An obnoxious me emerged. I kept pestering the nurses to find the resident and get an order for more anti-nausea drugs. I kept calling Jeremy and asking if he had spoken to his friend, the gastroenterologist, and maybe he had some idea what could be wrong.

At some point, I thought we were about to have a GI consult because a guy walked in and introduced himself as Dr. Somebody and that he was here to talk about good nutrition. Was he for real? I know it was not nice of me, but I asked him to leave. We had to control the vomiting so Matt could eat something, anything, nutritious or not. I told this guy I would be glad to speak with him when Matt was better but not a moment sooner.

He said, "Suit yourself. It's your loss."

I said I would take my chances, and he stormed out of the room and slammed the door. Matt was staring at me. He told me later that he had never seen me become so assertive, and he worried that he surely must be dying if I was so concerned.

We still had no answer, and Matt continued to vomit. After about ten days and a weight loss of fifteen or more pounds, Dr. Mozingo and Jeremy were speaking on the phone. Dr. Mozingo said, "I know what's wrong with Matt. I've seen it in a couple other patients before. He has SMA syndrome."

Okay, but now just what is SMA syndrome? The superior mesenteric artery sits on a fat pad above the duodenum, and when one loses the fat pad, the artery collapses onto the duodenum, which acts like a band compressing the duodenum, thus creating a duodenal blockage. Thank goodness we had the diagnosis. Now we needed a course of action. Matt would be taken to radiology, and a long tube would be put down his nose. The length was such that it went beyond the blocked area so he could start receiving food and calories that way. The bucket behind his head started to be less full, and the nurses were emptying it less frequently, but Matt was still very weak and now only weighed seventy-six pounds. On, or about, the eighteenth of August, Matt went the entire day without vomiting and said he had no nausea. Tricia and I were hugging and kissing him and having a good time with Matt when a nurse whom I had never met before came in and started reprimanding us.

He said, "Keep your hands off my patient! You're both touching him, and you're filthy!"

And I thought, *Who the hell is this egomaniac?*

It turned out he had been a nurse in the burn unit but had taken a leave of absence, and that day was his first day back on the job. I guess it was important for him to throw his weight around.

I heard one of the doctors say to him, "Don't ever speak to a patient's family member like that again. These folks have been here for five months now, and they know the rules!"

I think the reprimand came from Dr. Mozingo, but I am not sure. Tricia and I did have on our yellow smocks and surgical gloves, but I was very hot and failed to wrap the smock around my waist, and it was open.

A few minutes later, the nurse came in to apologize, but I ignored him. When he walked out, Matt, always the nice guy, said, "He's just doing his job, Mom."

And I said, "And I'm just doing mine!"

Matt said, "Okay."

Today was also Tricia's twenty-seventh birthday, so Matt said the two of us should go out for a nice dinner. I took her to the Melting Pot in Gainesville, which was her favorite fondue restaurant. It was a strained dinner because I was getting the impression that Tricia was tired of being with us, and she had a lot of mood swings. One day she would be fine and talkative, and the next day she was angry and pouting. I told her what I was observing and said I understood how hard this was on her since she was spending more time with me than with Matt, and I did not know how to handle this either.

When we got home to the apartment Tricia told me she was sure of two things: her man and her love for him and the invitations she wanted to send out for their wedding.

She called Matt her "Little man" because she was about two inches taller, and she said, "Mom Cole, if I don't marry Matt, I'll never marry anyone else. I love Matt too much!"

I thought, *What great words, but time will tell.*

The next morning, we entered the burn unit and once again were told it was moving day. Yard Dog was packing up Matt's belongings and told us he would accompany us down the hall. We had no idea where we were going but finally learned we were moving down the hall to the general medicine ward.

Matt said, "Is that good?"

I supposed any time a patient left the burn unit, that was good.

Once again we busied ourselves with settling into a room. And once again the familiar entourage came into Matt's room. All the nurses from the burn unit stopped by at the end of their shifts, and Jeff and Eddie found Matt to do PT and OT on his legs and arms.

I had regressed to a point where I was crying all the time again, but, to coin Matt's phrase, "They were happy tears." I knew discharge was around the corner, but no one had said anything to us yet. Tricia went back to work, which left Matt and me alone once again to talk about life. He said he was so frightened and did not want to talk about going home, because what would become of his life? He said he had no way to support Tricia or a family. Even though they had discussed reversing roles—Tricia said she was willing to work and support them while Matt could be Mr. Mom—I knew he would not like that arrangement, but Matt kept quiet and I said nothing to him.

We continued to spend time together in his room on the ward, and I kept telling Matt he did not have a head injury and could accomplish anything. I started to believe myself, too.

On a very stormy and rainy Friday night, Matt said he wanted to take a walk around the ward, so I helped him out of bed, put on the hospital bathrobe and his slippers, and off we went. I also had to make sure the tube down his nose was intact, and checking that and unwinding it took more time than making sure he was dressed and ready. We walked slowly down the ward, and, of course, stopped at the nurses' station to talk to everyone. Matt was receiving plenty of kudos, and he loved every moment of the attention. I believe he was very proud of his accomplishments, and he thrived on all the positive comments that were thrown in his direction.

When we came to the window at the end of the hall, Matt looked down at the city of Gainesville. We had a great view because we were on the seventh floor. Suddenly, Matt burst into tears and was crying uncontrollably. I had no idea, yet, that he was looking at his own reflection in the window. His hair had been shaved off, and a patch of skin had been used for a chin graft, his ears were gone, his right eye was pulling down and needed another graft, and his bottom lip looked enormously swollen, although what was happening was the lip was turning outward as the burns were healing.

As I looked at my own reflection, I saw a very sad lady. My hair had grown a lot and needed a good trim, my face was thinner, I had bags under my eyes, I had developed deep grooves around my mouth that were not there before, and I, too, was a mess.

We stood there for a few minutes, I with my arm around Matt, and then we turned around and slowly walked back to his room. Even though we had probably walked no more than fifty feet, Matt was exhausted. I helped him into bed, covered him up, and sat down in the easy chair to rest. We had progressed to a point where I could leave in the evening and he would not be terrified. I always put the nurses call button close to his right foot so he could use it if he had to, and I left his door ajar so he could bear activity in the hall. Matt told me that he was able to sleep on and off at night and was not quite so frightened. He still preferred that Tricia or I stay with him, but he understood that we were not allowed to now that he was on the ward.

I was feeling better now that Matt was recovering, but I still had trouble sleeping, and I thought a lot about Jeremy and my two girls who were left behind in Los Angeles. I would fall asleep wondering what it was going to feel like to sleep in my own bed and wake up to Southern California sunshine. I daydreamed a lot about sitting on my back patio with Jeremy and enjoying a cup of cappuccino, something we did often. I could feel the head of one of my Labs in my lap, and I could feel the velvety softness of an ear. But then I would be awakened and realize that no one had discussed going home yet. I would just have to wait and put my daydreams on the back burner.

CHAPTER
NINE

Tricia and I continued to visit Matt and spend time with him daily. I still brought lunch in for him every day, and we would eat together. Matt had to be fed by either Tricia or me, but I had the sense he no longer cared. He was just very grateful to be alive, and he appreciated our help.

On August 25, a new resident came onto the ward. This was his first rotation after graduating from medical school. His name was Eric, and he was a very handsome young man, but also a very insecure fellow. We called him Dr. Eric, and if I ever asked him a question, he would say, "I'll get back to you," and then disappear.

One afternoon, I was helping Matt in the bathroom, and as we were making our way back to his bed, his NG tube slipped out of his nose and fell at our feet. Matt and I came to a stop and just stared at it.

Matt said, "Mom, quick. Wipe it off and put it back down my nose!"

I quickly said I had no idea how to put an NG tube down someone's nose, and furthermore, I am not a nurse.

He said, "How hard can it be? Besides, if we call for help, it will take them ages to get here!"

I explained to him that the nurses were very busy, probably had two or three patients to take care of, and it was difficult for them to answer a patient's call button immediately. Matt said it sure was different to be on the ward. I think he was missing the attention of the nurses on the burn unit, but, of course, the ward was a lot different. Everyone on the ward would be going home eventually, including us, whereas, quite a few patients never left the burn unit.

Matt's NG tube did, indeed, lay on his end table for about eight hours. No one checked on us, and Dr. Eric was not around all day. Matt was eating and drinking on his own. He felt fine, and there was no nausea. He was in no danger without the tube.

Finally the doctor came in and laughed. He said to me, "Mom Cole, did you DC the NG tube?"

I said, "No. It DC'd itself!"

He picked it up and said Matt did not really need it anymore and he would dispose of it.

Matt promptly started to cry and said, "Do you know how good it feels to have that damn hose out of my nose?"

I was thrilled for Matt, so I joined in the crying session. We had never been so emotional before, and I wondered what had happened to us. It was obvious we had a lot of adjusting to do, but right now I just felt like reveling in the demise of the NG tube.

On Wednesday night of that week, Dr. Eric decided Matt needed an IV and he would call for the phlebotomist to come and put it in his foot. Matt was very upset, and I had questions for the doctor. I said Matt was drinking plenty of fluids and was urinating on his own and was most likely not dehydrated. Dr. Eric and I had no way of knowing how many ounces of fluid Matt was drinking. I said that I certainly did because I was the person who never left Matt's bedside and would hold the straw for him while he drank water, sweet tea, juice, or soda. I also accompanied him to the bathroom and helped him. I knew what he was eliminating, and I knew he was not dehydrated, but I was not there to argue with the resident.

An hour or so later, a beautiful young lady arrived with all her IV paraphernalia and told us she would now start the IV in Matt's left foot. She proceeded to poke the foot endlessly, and I listened to Matt's screams as I paced the hall.

Dr. Eric finally said to me, "She's the best in the hospital."

I said, "Maybe she should take a refresher course!"

I said before that I had turned into an obnoxious me. I felt that Matt had survived burns over 65 percent of his body, the worst injuries a body could sustain, and now he had to endure more torment while this gal looked for a vein. I walked into Matt's room and asked her to leave. She seemed relieved as she picked up her tray and quickly left. I told Dr. Eric I would stay with Matt all night and make sure he drank enough water. I would make sure Matt did not become dehydrated, but Dr. Eric said that would not be necessary and I should go home and get a good night's sleep.

Of course, I had no sleep at all. I was very worried about Matt and his dehydration, which I still felt was nonexistent. I was worried about his ability to get out of bed and go to the bathroom if he had to. I worried about his ability to hold his water cup if he were thirsty, and, naturally, I worried about going home. I was anxious to see my husband and my girls, I wanted to pet my dogs and see my friends, and I wanted to sleep in my own bed and feel the security of having Jeremy next to me. Still there was no word about discharge.

On Friday evening, August 31st, Dr. Eric walked in with a tray that had blue gloves on it, but I could not see what else was on the tray because the gloves were covering the contents.

Matt, Tricia, and I looked at each other, and I know we all thought, *Now what?*

Dr. Eric must have known we were anxious, so he became very animated, something we had never seen, and said, "Guess what tomorrow is?"

Matt said, "I can't guess. What's going on?"

And much to our shock, the doctor said, "You're going home tomorrow!"

I almost screamed. Tricia and Matt were hugging, and I was jumping up and down.

Eric said, "Easy does it, folks. Let's get rid of the NG tube and IV," which had both been reinserted two days prior, "and make sure Matt can walk."

Matt said, "Are you kidding, man? I'm outta here! Thanks for everything, but I'm on my way!"

By now we were all laughing and crying and hugging Matt and getting ready to pack his belongings and be on our way. Dr. Eric said discharge would be Saturday morning, September 1, 2001, exactly five and a half months after the accident.

Tricia and I went home that night, and neither of us slept. At 3:00 a.m., I wandered out to the kitchen, where Tricia found me for tea. We assumed Matt was wide awake also. This event was monumental and a great milestone in Matt's recovery. I told Tricia we had better get some sleep because in a few hours we would be bringing Matt to my apartment and we would get ready for the long trip home. Home—that was the sweetest word I had ever heard.

CHAPTER
TEN

Saturday morning dawned bright and beautiful in Gainesville, and Tricia and I were out the door by 9:00 a.m. Adrenaline was running high at that point, and all I could think about was my child and getting him discharged from the hospital.

When we arrived in Matt's room, his bed was empty. Dr. Eric said he saw Matt running down the hall a few moments ago.

"Where was he going?" I asked.

"Probably to the shower room," I was told.

Up until that moment, I had no idea the shower room was two floors below us.

Tricia and I busied ourselves with Matt's belongings. She pulled down his posters and family photos, and I packed his suitcase. As I folded his shirts and socks, I held each piece of clothing for a moment and gave thanks to the Lord for saving Matt. I really could not think straight. Now I was generally preoccupied with Matt's recovery once we arrived in Los Angeles.

One of the nurses came in and told us the reporter had arrived. I had no idea what she was talking about, nor did Tricia, so we waited. Matt returned from his shower and was dressed in new comfy pants, a soft shirt, socks, and his new slip-on sneakers. Tricia and I had purchased everything for him at Target, but I was sure he was not fond of his new attire since he was dressed like his grandfather. Matt laughed and understood that I was looking for comfort and something he could easily put on and take off.

He said, "I won't be in Grandpa-styled clothes for long!"

At that point, the reporter from the *Daytona Beach Newspaper* came into Matt's room. With him was a photographer. They introduced themselves and told us they had initially done the story for the paper at the time of the accident and they wanted to write another follow-up story and take pictures on "going home" day. I never asked them how they knew it was the big day. I just went along with the interview. I was asked how I was planning to care for Matt once we arrived in Los Angeles. I told the reporter it would be no big deal because Matt was an important part of our family, my firstborn, my only son, and I had no problem helping him.

Matt, Tricia, and I walked with the cameraman to the burn unit, where we had our picture taken and once again said goodbye to everyone. Bruce was not there, but Yard Dog gave us his phone number and made us promise to keep in touch. Sue Mary and Jody gave us their numbers and e-mail addresses and told me to report often on Matt's recovery. We said we would always be friends as we hugged everyone one last time. And then the most amazing thing happened. It was an occurrence that I will never forget. We walked out of the burn unit, slammed the door behind us, and kept walking. None of us looked back. As we made our way around the corner, I was the first one to fall apart, then Matt and then Tricia. The three of us just stood in the hall and hugged and cried uncontrollably. I was holding Matt so tightly I thought I might squash him, but he never complained or squirmed. He just let me hold on to him. I felt pressure on my back and shoulders and realized that he and Tricia were holding onto me as tightly as I had a grip on them. The photographer kept snapping pictures, but I told him this was private time with my kids and not for anyone to see. Gratefully none of those photos ever appeared in the newspaper.

In Matt's room one last time, Matt was put in a wheelchair while Tricia went downstairs to get the car. We would wait for her in front of the hospital. The nurse accompanied us down the elevator and into the lobby. As we walked to the front door, I realized everyone was staring at Matt, but he held his head up high and said, "Hello, how are you" to everyone. The nurse said it was very warm outside and we should wait inside, but Matt nixed that idea.

He said, "You know, I haven't smelled the air for almost six months. Let's go outside."

When we wheeled Matt outside, he said to me, "Mom, is this really happening? Are you really taking me home?"

I said we were, indeed, leaving Shands Hospital and would be on our way to Los Angeles in a few days.

Matt said to me, "What if I don't make it outside the burn unit? What if I have to come back?"

I said, "Matt, that is not an option."

He said, "Says who?"

I said, "I say so!"

He said, "Well then, let's go!"

Matt always had the ability to make me smile, and this time was no different. When Tricia drove up with the car, Matt and I were acting silly, and, as he said, he was drunk on sunshine. I had never heard a more apropos description.

We loaded Matt into the front seat, buckled his seat belt, and put all his belongings in the trunk. Tricia turned up the radio, and we drove off while listening to OutKast's "So Fresh, So Clean." Tricia was singing, I was clapping, and Matt was bobbing his head up and down. Oh, what a curious threesome we must have been! But it was our day! If anyone would ask me what day in my life stands out, I would have to say that, after my wedding day, and the days my children were born, September 1, 2001 will always be remembered as the day I took Matt home.

Matt was surprised to learn that my apartment was only one mile from the hospital. We had stopped for sandwiches at Matt's favorite Florida sub-shop and then we headed for the home I had lived in for the past five and a half months.

We parked the car and walked into my building lobby, where we were greeted by Stan, the doorman.

He ran up to Matt and said, "Son, you have no idea how much I've heard about you. Your Mom has told me about you, and I'm honored to meet you!"

Matt said, "I'm honored to meet you, sir. Thank you for keeping my mom safe."

Stan started to cry. That was the first of many times I would witness the effect Matt had on others.

When we opened the door to my sixth-floor apartment, Matt looked around and said, "So this is where you have been living?"

I said, "Yes, I've been here since the first part of April."

Matt was emotional again and said, "Thanks for hanging around in Gainesville and being in charge of all the goings-on!"

I said, "That's what moms do."

Matt just laughed.

I had left my slippers by the couch, and my book and glasses were on the coffee table alongside my empty teacup.

Matt started to cry again as he said, "There is so much evidence of you being here. Do you mind if I slip my shoes off and leave them on the floor?"

I said my house was now his house for the few days before we would head for home, so he could enjoy his time with me and do what he wanted.

I had never seen such an emotional Matt. I felt every time I said something, he would start to sniffle. I knew he was having a tough time and was extremely frightened to be out of the hospital. I knew he was worried about succeeding in the outside world once again, but I felt, with time, Matt would be fine.

We three had a simple chicken dish I prepared for dinner and then we watched TV and talked late into the night. It seemed as if we all had a lot to say to each other. We had always had someone in the hospital room with us, so it was our first chance to bare our souls to one another.

Matt said when he had jumped out of the burning plane, he had no idea if he could put out the flames on his body, so he rolled on the ground. The flames were very stubborn and kept on burning him. He said he felt someone push him down, throw something over his shoulder, and keep patting his shoulders and back. Matt said he remembered the sirens getting closer, and he knew when the paramedics cut off his clothes and shoes. He also said he remembered the paramedic telling him that he would give him a shot to "put him to sleep." For some strange reason, Matt thought he was about to be euthanized. He said at that moment he was in so much pain he did not care, and euthanasia sounded appealing to him.

He said, "However, before you put me to sleep, please tell my family how much I have loved them!"

He said the paramedic responded, "Good luck, young man, and may God bless you!"

I had no idea Matt had such vivid memories of what happened, and once again I was upset.

Tricia said she remembered calling me right after she had heard about the accident, but, much to her surprise, I already knew what had happened. She said she worried about how to tell me about Matt's accident, but she said, as soon as I answered the phone and she heard my voice, she knew I was aware of everything.

Matt told us he remembered everything about the crash and the events that took place beforehand. He remembered the fear he felt when he realized the plane was going down, but he could not get any words out to express his feeling.

I was very upset to know my child had to feel such fear, the fear that death might be upon him.

Our emotions were really bouncing off the walls, and the three of us sobbed and hugged late into the night.

I went to bed, but Matt and Tricia stayed up to talk some more. I presumed they had a lot of catching up to do, and I wanted to leave them alone.

When I awoke early Sunday morning, the kids were still sleeping. I saw Matt's shoes on the floor and his duffel bag in the corner, and my heart stopped. I realized this would be the first Sunday in months that I would not be rushing to the burn unit. I hoped everyone in the unit had had a peaceful night, and I prayed there had been no new disastrous admissions.

We decided we would drive to Daytona Beach that afternoon because Matt wanted to pick up a few things from his apartment and take them home to California.

After lunch, Matt and Tricia got into his little Integra. I followed in her Honda, and we were on our way. About halfway to Daytona, I followed Tricia into a parking lot where there was an outdoor fruit stand. She said that Matt was very hot. He was agitated and had difficulty sitting because his decubitus site was aching. She thought we should stop and walk around for a few moments to give Matt some time to stretch.

We bought a bag of peaches and some tomatoes and then got into the cars to continue our drive to Daytona Beach. It was a beautiful Florida day, but it was hot and uncomfortable. I had the air conditioner going on high, and I hoped that Matt was alright in the car ahead of me.

When we arrived at Matt and Tricia's apartment complex, I had a very strange feeling. It was the feeling of great sadness, but at that point, I had no idea what was making me so sad.

As we climbed the stairs to the second-floor apartment, I realized that as much as Matt loved living here and enjoyed his independent life with Tricia, I knew he would never live here again. I think the uncertainty of the future was making me very morose, and I was extremely worried about Matt. On the one hand, I was euphoric that he survived; on the other hand, I felt, now what?

I caught Tricia's eye, and she, too, was feeling something because her beautiful blue eyes were filled with tears.

We rested in the apartment for a while and then Matt and Tricia started to pack some of their clothes and get ready for our long trek to Los Angeles. We all heard the doorbell and were pleasantly surprised to see Francois standing by the door.

Francois, also, was recovering nicely from the crash. He had had a compression fracture of his back, and he would continue to wear the back brace for the next few months. He brought the ubiquitous bag of candy for Matt, and he hugged Matt over and over again.

Francois was thrilled to see Matt upright and walking. After all, he had seen Matt only lying in bed for the past six months.

After Francois visited with us for a while, he left us with hugs, kisses, and promises to keep in touch. Matt thanked him for the candy and said he would have something to munch on while we drove home, but that never happened. Matt had all the goodies eaten before we even left Gainesville.

Our next visitor was the young man who had been taking care of Matt and Tricia's dog, Tallahassee. He brought the dog to the apartment because the fifteen-pound fur-ball would be going back to California with us. Matt was very excited to see his little dog, and she climbed onto Matt's lap and stared at him for a few moments until she recognized his voice.

We all slept well that night, and Monday morning we were ready to pack most of Matt's clothes into the car and drive back to Gainesville. Tricia had decided to leave her car parked in the lot of the complex, so the three of us, along with the dog, squeezed into the Integra and headed for my own apartment. Tomorrow we had a lot of work to do. There would be packing and an RV to pick up. I had to tie up some loose ends with our building manager, and I needed to buy some products to clean the apartment.

Monday night we made plans to go to a sushi restaurant and meet some of our friends for dinner. The first to arrive was Matt's loyal friend and fellow pilot, Paddy Hyndman. The guys were so excited to see each other. They hugged over and over, and Paddy ignored Matt's tears. He was very cool about the emotional Matt.

Our other friends from the hospital came, and we were having a wonderful time when Matt made a noise that was similar to a scream.

He said to me, "Who was that?"

I looked around and saw no one, but standing at the front entrance was Matt's sister Leah.

There was more hugging and crying and stares from other customers. The couple sitting behind us asked what was happening, and I briefly told them this was a send-off for Matt by his friends and we would be on our way tomorrow. They wished us well and said they would pray for Matt's continued recovery. Matt was shocked that

Leah was sitting next to him. We quickly bought her some food and after long goodbyes, headed for my apartment.

My little apartment was crowded because at the last minute, we decided to take Matt's Integra back to California with us and Paddy would drive behind our rented RV. Leah had taken time off from work to drive back with us, too. Between Tricia, Leah, and me, Matt was in very loving hands, but I was apprehensive about the long drive home. We did not have a GPS (global positioning system) in our RV, and I was worried about finding a hospital along the I-10 if we needed one. I knew I was getting ahead of myself, but I was unable to shake this feeling that something could happen.

The next morning we all woke up to sunshine and warmth and Matt's voice saying, "What's for breakfast?"

We decided to have Krispy Kreme doughnuts, so we sent Paddy to the store to pick up the delicacies for us. I had to make coffee about five times because I had a small pot and it did not hold enough coffee for all of us.

After a non-nutritious breakfast, I gave Leah my credit card, and she and Tricia went to pick up the RV. Paddy sat and kept Matt company while I started putting my belongings in boxes.

When the girls returned, I was shocked to see the size of the RV they had rented. It was monstrous. Tricia said Matt needed to be comfortable, and we would use the space for all our belongings. That was true, but I had no idea if I could drive this RV. I am not very tall, and as it worked out, I could not reach the pedals. Leah assured me that she and Tricia would do the driving and there was no need to worry.

We stopped at the local Walmart and picked up cleaning supplies to spruce up the apartment. I was rarely there, and I never made a mess. I always cleaned up after myself, and there was little to do.

Before I started to clean, I had to give Matt his shower and do burn wound care on his legs. Tricia and I were doing Matt's legs together, and he was complaining that he was very hot and comfortable. We put his Bermuda shorts on, but I could certainly see how he could be so hot. He had elastic stockings on his legs, and underneath that we wound gauze around his thin legs, which had been slathered with Silvadene ointment. His donor sites were not healing, and he said his legs were throbbing. On top of that, Matt said he was so hot that he felt faint. I turned down the air conditioner a few more degrees and told Matt to lie on the couch for a few minutes.

As he was sitting down on the couch, he lost his balance and somehow fell backward onto the couch, landing on his left hand. Tricia called me quietly, and when I came into the room, I saw that she was gently holding Matt's hand. She said they needed a towel immediately. I gave it to her, and she wrapped Matt's hand. He was white and looked like he was about to faint. His left ring finger had bent back when he sat on his hand, and the finger was dangling by a thin piece of skin. There was hardly any bleeding because as I said, the blood supply in his arms and hands was severely compromised, but we needed to have the finger sewn back on.

Tricia called the hospital, and they told us to get an ambulance and have him brought to the emergency room. I said, hell no. We had just spent five and a half months in this hospital, and I expected better service than waiting in an ER for ten hours.

The ambulance did take Matt to the hospital, and the driver did attempt to leave Matt at the ER, but I said we would not sit in the ER.

He said, "Well, ma'am, you're on your own!"

I said fine. Matt, Tricia, Leah, and I walked into the hospital and rode up the elevator to the burn unit on the seventh floor. The burn clinic was in session, so we walked down the hallway and knocked on the door. We were greeted by the resident who was in charge of the burn clinic, and he heartily welcomed Matt and said he would sew the finger back on. Matt was given a shot of an antibiotic of some sort, and we had a prescription for more antibiotics. The finger was sewn back on and wrapped in layers of gauze, but we knew we had to be very careful so we would have no more mishaps.

We were only gone from the apartment for about two hours, and we returned at dinnertime. The first one to announce his hunger was Matt.

We sent Paddy to the Olive Garden to pick up food, and we quickly ate our meal in the RV. After eating, I ran upstairs to collect all my belongings and brought them down to the RV. We parked under a tree so the sun would not beat down on the roof because Matt was sitting in the RV with Tallahassee and reading his book. It took fifteen trips up to the apartment to get all the boxes I had packed. I had accumulated more junk than I realized.

After moving all my boxes into the RV, it was time to clean. As I said before, Tricia and I were the only ones in the apartment, and we were both very neat. There was not much to be done, so we finished the house cleaning in record time. As I closed and locked the door, I realized a new chapter in my life was beginning. I had no idea how things would go once we arrived home in Los Angeles. I was aware of the trauma that had attacked my family, and I knew that life as we knew it had come to an end the day Matt had his accident. But I was ready for the challenge. I was going home and was taking Matt with me. That was something that was an uncertainty a few months earlier. I was still standing in the apartment building hallway when I heard a horn honking in the parking lot. That brought me back to my senses, so I got into the elevator and went downstairs. I gave the keys to Stan, who would give them to the building manager in the morning, and after handshakes, hugs, and goodbyes, I climbed into the RV with Leah, Tricia, and Matt.

Paddy was in the Integra ready to drive behind us. Leah put on the radio and drove out the parking lot and headed for the I-95. We would pick up I-10 in Jacksonville, but that was almost one hundred miles away. It was already eight o'clock at night, and I was getting tired. Matt was lying on the couch in the back of the RV, and Tricia was sitting next to him. Leah was driving, and I was sitting up front with her. We were talking to each other, and, of course, we were discussing how different life would be once we got home. I kept saying over and over how frightened I was and worried that my perfectly run household would be topsy-turvy. I told Leah I felt we had no choice but to take one step and one day at a time. We would see how that would go and take it from there.

We were all very tired from our exciting day, and we only drove a little beyond Jacksonville, Florida. We were only on the road for two hours but were too exhausted to continue. We checked into a Holiday Inn and were lucky enough to get two adjoining rooms.

Before getting into bed, Tricia and I did wound care on Matt's legs and gave him all his medications. I told Paddy to be sure to wake me up if Matt had any kind of problem. I heard Tricia going out the door a few times during the night, and I knew she was checking on Tallahassee, who was asleep in the RV.

At 8:05 a.m. I felt someone tapping my shoulder and saying, "Mom, wake up! I'm hungry and it's time to get on the road."

I opened my eyes and saw my skinny little boy standing by my side. Oh, he looked so thin and frail, but he was hungry so that was a good sign.

We all ate a hearty breakfast and were ready to get on the road. Matt was doing well and said he felt fine. He reported that he slept really well and had a dream about his room in California. I now had to tell him that we were not going to our house in Tarzana, but were going to our rental house in Toluca Lake. He started to cry. He had forgotten that our house in Tarzana had been sold, and he was in his drug-induced coma when we rented the new house. I do not remember telling him that the sale of the Tarzana house had gone through, and honestly, I forgot to bring up moving when we would discuss things in the hospital. Matt said he could not imagine going to another house to live in. He said he was attached to our house in Tarzana since we had lived there since he was four years old. I explained that the Tarzana house was just too big for our family now, and life will go on nicely for all of us in different surroundings.

Matt said, "Okay. I'll give it a try in the new house!"

Oh boy.

Ahead of us, I could see Interstate 10. I swear if I had a pair of binoculars, I could see all the way to California. None of the kids believed me, and Matt said to buckle up because we had a long drive ahead of us.

Since we were all settled down in the RV, Leah buckled her seat belt, I sat next to her with Tallahassee in my lap, Matt and Tricia were in the back, and I could see that Matt was dozing off. Ahead lay the I-10. We were finally homeward bound.

CHAPTER
ELEVEN

Matt was born on July 1, 1977, at 8:54 a.m. He only weighed six pounds eight ounces, and, truth be told, he resembled a plucked chicken. He had thin arms and spindly legs, and all in all he was a very little guy.

Initially Matt's eyes were some sort of blue color, but by four months, they were dark brown, exactly like mine. And he hated to sleep. I would feed him, bathe him, burp him, and spend hours rocking him. The second I would lay him down in his crib, the eyes would fly open, the mouth would open, and out came the screams. At night he would scream and grunt and scream some more. I never knew what he wanted. At about five months, I had the bright idea to bring him into bed with me. He immediately fell asleep and slept until the morning. Jeremy and I took a lot of criticism for that, but I'm glad I had my own ideas. Letting him into our bed worked for us. The three of us were sleeping well and waking up refreshed. At about nine months, I very easily transferred him to his crib, and he had no problem staying there. That, however, was short-lived because on his first birthday, he decided to climb out of his crib. Actually, I think he fell out because we heard his screams, and when we ran to his room, he was sitting on the floor and rubbing his head.

My heart stopped when I saw him out of his crib because at this point, I was seven months pregnant and was worried I would never have the chance to sleep through the night again.

Matt was very persistent. He would climb out of his crib, run to our room, stand over me, and lift my eyelid, saying, "Mommy! Hi!"

I was very crabby with him because I just wanted to sleep. But I always took him back to his crib, would tell him how much I loved him, how tired Mommy and Daddy were, and we would see him in the morning. Good night.

To no avail was all my great consistency. He had more energy than I did and continued to climb out of his crib.

On the night of September 27, 1978, he came out of his crib thirty-two times.

Jeremy and I were exhausted.

Thankfully I had a bit of a respite because on September 28, 1978, our daughter Leah was born, and I had two wonderful nights in the hospital.

When I came home with Matt's new baby sister, he stopped in his tracks and pointed at her. I showed him the baby, but he just ran away. My mother, who had been staying with Matt, bought him a huge Tonka dump truck, and he was much more interested in that than his sister.

On the evening of October 1, 1978, I washed Leah, fed her, and put her to sleep. She slept until 1:00 p.m. the next day. As usual, I was up with Matt, but our new infant slept through the night.

I have often said how nature took such good care of me because my oldest child was not sleeping, but my new baby loved to sleep. I just cannot imagine how I would have managed if the two of them were awake.

Matt was not speaking, and he was almost two. He said, "Mommy," "Daddy," "Twinkie" (the dog), "Grandma Dorothy" (my mother), but nothing else. Now I was worried why he only pointed his finger or would walk up to the refrigerator, tap the door, and grunt. Really, I knew what he wanted, but I sure did wish he would talk.

Right after Matt's third birthday, I enrolled him at Temple Ahavat Shalom Nursery School. He would go three days a week from 9:00 a.m. until noon. The first day I took him, he cried when I was leaving. He latched onto my leg and would not let go. The teacher said to leave and he would be fine. I am glad I was not one of those moms who hover because I walked out after hugs and kisses. I knew the teacher could handle this much better than I could, so I felt comfortable leaving Matt in her capable hands.

When I returned to pick him up at noon, the teacher opened the door and gave quick feedback to all the moms who were anxiously waiting. She said Matt had done just fine. He stopped crying as soon as I left, and he and a little boy named Gregory played side by side all morning. They even shared the blocks, trucks, and puzzles. I was very pleased to receive such a glowing report on the first day of school, but we had a slight problem. Matt was down on the floor on all fours, and he was barking like a dog. When I greeted him, he barked at me. I thought, *Now what the heck is wrong with my kid?* Once I got him out of the classroom, he was fine. Still he was not speaking.

I had shared my concern with the teacher about a week later, and she said there are quite a few kids who cannot, or will not, speak until they are good and ready. I hoped Matt was one of them.

About the middle of October, right after Leah had turned two, I was in the kitchen chopping vegetables for soup when someone said, "Mommy, I would really like it if you prepared me a tuna sandwich."

I looked around. Leah had fallen asleep on the couch while watching Mr. Rogers, and Twinkie, the family Schnoodle, was fast asleep on the carpet.

Matt was standing close by and was looking up at me. He said, "Tuna is my favorite!"

I was shocked.

He said, "Don't look so surprised, Mommy. I actually have a good vocabulary!"

Now I really was shocked. I was hugging him and twirling him around the kitchen. I said, We must call Dad to give him the good news."

Matt said, "Fine. But I'll speak!"

From that day on, Matt never stopped talking. What's more, he always spoke grammatically correct, and he did, indeed, have a great vocabulary. To this day, I have no idea what took him so long to speak. I guess he was waiting for that tuna sandwich.

When Matt turned seven, he told his grandfather that someday when he grew up, he would like to be a pilot and fly the heavy iron. I had no idea he knew that expression, but he must have heard it somewhere. He loved to fly to New York to see his grandparents, and he especially loved flying across the Pacific Ocean for Hawaii. Those were the days when the captain would let Matt and his dad into the cockpit to see all the controls and look out the window. For Matt, that was the highlight of the trip.

Through the year, Matt talked about taking flying lessons and one day being in charge of the heavy iron. This conversation came up many times while Matt was growing up.

Our years with Matt as a teenager were relatively quiet. He was a very mellow, laid-back guy, and he was very well behaved and always had the best manners. He loved sushi and pizza but was probably the only American kid who was not fond of spaghetti. He liked the sauce and the meatballs, but not the pasta.

We continued to take two or three trips a year to our favorite Hawaiian island, Kauai, and we all loved to choose a special place for our yearly ski trip.

Matt was the extreme skier in the family. He loved the black diamond slopes, and he would try to traverse every mogul be could find. Our girls were much more cautious, as was Jeremy, because they were afraid of getting injured.

During the summer that Matt turned sixteen, Jeremy came home and said he had a patient named Dan, who was a flight instructor at Van Nuys Airport. Maybe this coming weekend he would take Matt and Jeremy for a flight. Matt was so excited, and he talked about the upcoming event for about four or five days. Thankfully, Dan was free, and he did take the guys on that flight. They met at Van Nuys Airport and flew up the coast to Santa Barbara. Then they came inland and flew South over LAX and Long Beach. When they came home, they monopolized the conversation with their flight and which VOR they passed and which 747 they saw landing at LAX. And, by the way, Matt was signed up with Dan for his first flight lesson Wednesday after school. I had known this was coming.

Flight lesson day came around very quickly, and Matt, who was in eleventh grade, wanted to stay home from school and prepare for his lesson. I said absolutely not. School came first, flying lessons second. I said his responsibility was to get good grades, and Dad and I would pay for lessons. He rolled his eyes at me and reluctantly went to school.

He went to the Van Nuys Airport right after his last class because even though the airport was just a few miles from our house, he was worried he might be late.

He finally arrived home at about seven and said he was very hungry. We had waited for him to have dinner, so we all sat down together to talk about our day and enjoy our meal. Matt was flying high, literally and figuratively. He was so excited. The words were flowing out of his mouth nonstop. He told us about ground school and learning about the instruments and air speed and straight and level climbs and turns. And then his time in the plane was applying everything he had just learned while at the same time looking out at the horizon and watching for other aircraft. He was thoroughly hooked and was anxiously awaiting next week's lesson.

Matt continued to take lessons from Dan for the next few months until mid-March 1994. He came home from an afternoon lesson, and he was missing the back part of his tee shirt. I was shocked because I knew he had just completed his solo flight. He was so excited, but mostly he was very proud of his accomplishment. He also had some bad news. Dan had been hired by a corporate company and would no longer be Matt's instructor.

Although Matt was nervous about starting with a new teacher, that did not deter him. The next week he was back at the airport and met Alan Goldsman, who would take over where Dan left off.

It was a match made in heaven. Matt excelled and was learning great things from Alan. And they got along famously.

For the next eight to nine months Matt would meet with Alan. Sometimes they would just do ground school, and sometimes they would just fly the airplane.

When Matt started twelfth grade in September 1994, he finished his school day at noon. I was working in Jeremy's office, and Matt called to say he was preparing for his solo cross-country flight that afternoon. I really had no idea what that meant, so Jeremy had to explain it to me. It meant, simply, that the pilot must fly to three separate points a minimum of fifty nautical miles from the original airport. Matt said he would call us as soon as he arrived wherever he was going. That made me nervous, but Jeremy said Matt was competent, conscientious, and cautious and he would be fine. Well, I was busy working in the afternoon but also was staring at the phone waiting for Matt's call. He finally called and said he had had quite an afternoon. He left Van Nuys Airport at about one in the afternoon and headed for Santa Maria. After landing there, he went to the Mexican restaurant at the airport and had three tacos and a Coke. He took off from Santa Maria and was headed for Porterville, which is close to Bakersfield, when he got lost. He could not find the airport, nor could he see the runway. The tower kept giving him instructions, which obviously he did not understand, because he said it took him forty-five minutes, and finally he spotted the runway. He told us he was so relieved.

We had a hearty laugh at his expense when we all gathered for dinner that night, but Matt loved the teasing he received from all of us.

Matt continued to fly 8231 Tango, a single-engine Cherokee Warrior, and we all enjoyed his Sunday afternoon flights. Jeremy and I loved to fly to Santa Maria or Santa Barbara and hug the beautiful Pacific Coast and look down at the ocean beneath us. Or sometimes we flew to Harris Ranch, near Bakersfield, and would have a quick lunch and then buy a few steaks for dinner along with some dessert. Oh, we loved those flights.

I remember one particular flight that took us further away from home than usual. The three of us climbed into the plane and headed down to San Diego. I had no idea how busy Lindbergh Field would be, but Matt made a slick landing in between two Southwest 737s.

We took a cab to my favorite seafood restaurant on Harbor Island and had dinner. After a cab ride to the San Diego Airport, we flew back to Van Nuys. It had been a beautiful Southern California day and also a day that I still remember very clearly and with great joy.

We always called Matt "Cautious Cal" because he was very conservative and never reckless. He was always a very competent and careful driver, so when Matt would be going out with his friends, his dad and I felt better if he were the guy behind the wheel. It was the same in the airplane. When the three of us would be. on a flight, I always sat in the back seat. That gave me the chance to watch the beautiful California scenery and also to daydream a little. It always amazed me to see Matt in charge of the plane and the controls and the radio. He also had his parents' lives in his hands, but he was very confident in the cockpit and his dad and I felt safe and always loved our time in the air with Matt.

We continued to fly with Matt as often as we could. The next year and a half passed uneventfully until it was time for Matt to leave home and move to Vero Beach, Florida, to attend Flight Safety International.

His time in Vero Beach was very productive, and he excelled at his work, plus made a lot of friends that are still in his life. It was a time of watching Matt grow up and turn into a very integritous adult as well as a very caring and generous young man. He was someone we were very proud of and loved unconditionally.

In early March, Matt and his dad met in Steamboat Springs, Colorado, for the yearly skiing trip, but we girls decided to forego skiing that year. Leah had just begun a new job with a pharmaceutical company, and Shayna was getting ready to graduate from high school. That was not the time to take off from work or school, so the boys had a wonderful time together. Jeremy still talks about the great week he had with his son but also sadly reminds me that he was the last one to see Matt healthy and whole before the accident. And how he wishes he would have told Matt to come back to California instead of flying in the opposite direction—to Florida where a life-changing event for all of us was just a week away.

CHAPTER
TWELVE

It was a long drive to Los Angeles, and I felt like we were not getting very far, but, of course we were making steady progress. As we drove through the outskirts of Tallahassee, Tricia pointed out a few things about her hometown. It was very windy at that point, and I was worried our RV would tip over, but luckily we stayed safe. We drove through Pensacola, where Matt announced, once again, he was hungry. We stopped at McDonald's, of course. Paddy Hyndman pulled into the parking lot in Matt's Integra and said that he, too, was starving. Looking at him, I remember thinking what a wonderful friend he was to Matt and how lucky we were to have him accompany us.

My plan for our road trip was to buy food and bring it into the RV to eat, sparing Matt's having to go into the restaurant. He nixed that idea.

He said, "I can walk, so let's go in and eat."

We had to bring him in a wheelchair because he was too weak to climb the RV stairs and walk into the restaurant. Paddy helped Matt and unfolded the wheelchair for us, and we were on our way. I hated the stares we got, and I resented people pointing at Matt like they had never seen an injured person before. After lunch, Matt said he had to use the restroom. We had discussed how we would handle that situation since Matt certainly needed help. I decided I would take him into the ladies' room, but first I would walk in and tell any ladies in the area that I was bringing in my son. In this particular restroom, there was an elderly lady with silver-blue hair who was standing in front of the mirror applying her lipstick.

I told her what I was about to do, and she said, "By all means, bring the boy in."

Well, I walked in with Matt, and she turned into Wacko Woman.

She said, "I've never seen such perversion in my life, and you are an A-1 pervert!"

I was shocked, to say the least, so I quickly shoved Matt into the stall. He did his business, and when we walked out of the stall, she was waiting for us. On and on she went.

"How dare you bring an adult male into the ladies' room?" And finally, "Lady, you are one crazy pig!"

After an afternoon of crying in the RV and wondering what I should do next time, I realized that she was the insensitive nasty old lady. After that, neither Jeremy nor I encountered anyone like that again. We continued to assist Matt in public bathrooms, and it was not any easier for Jeremy in the men's room. Guys do not like to see a man unzipping another guy's pants, but I think Jeremy was only questioned once about that. He explained that Matt was his son, had been in a terrible accident, and had lost the use of his hands. End of story. When I would walk into the restroom with Matt, most women would hug me and ask if they could help or if Matt or I needed anything. And how about prayers? Could they pray for Matt? That was something I never refused. All prayers, any denomination, would be accepted.

We continued our journey through a portion of Alabama, into Mississippi, and then into Louisiana. While coming closer to New Orleans, Leah received a phone call from one of our New York cousins saying that she had read the article about Matt's discharge from the hospital in the Daytona newspaper. And by the way, who is Tricia? Our cousin said the article had too much to say about the challenges Tricia was facing and none about Matt's parents and sisters. In fact, his sisters had no mention whatsoever. The East Coast family members were insulted. Just what I needed, I thought. At this point, I really was not worried about a newspaper article, nor was I worried about our New York cousins' interpretation of the article. Yes, I had been there. I answered questions and smiled for the camera, but I had no control over what had been written. Leah and I talked about this latest development and came to the conclusion we should not waste the time worrying about something we had no control over.

Coming into the city of New Orleans was very exciting. I had not been there for a long time, and I really loved the city. Leah had been there, also, and wanted to find a bakery where we could buy beignets, Matt had no idea what we were talking about, but the mere mention of a doughnut-like treat caught his attention.

We were driving through the French Quarter in a forty-two-foot RV, and we were a lot bigger than the sidewalk. Leah wanted those beignets, so we kept on driving. We were barely moving, so I suggested we move on and find the I-10 before we hit something, or God forbid someone. We stopped for gas, and I ran into the Food Mart and found the revered beignet mix. That was the best we could do. I put the box in the refrigerator with the promise to make the treats as soon as we got home.

That evening, we stopped at a restaurant for dinner. Leah, Tricia, and I took turns feeding Matt, and we all ate well. Leah said she was getting tired and maybe Tricia could drive for a bit. Tricia agreed, so we all got into the RV and drove off, with Paddy following behind us.

After driving for about forty-five minutes, Tricia said, "This is ridiculous!"

I had no idea what she was talking about, so I said, "What's wrong? What are you talking about?"

She said, "I'm exhausted. We need to find a hotel. Now."

We were in the middle of nowhere, and there was no hotel in sight, so I said, "Okay. The first hotel we see from the interstate, we'll stop at and get a room for the night."

I had the feeling Tricia was really annoyed, but Leah was having some quiet time with her brother, which she deserved, and Tricia did agree to do a portion of the driving.

I heard Matt and Leah laughing from the back of the RV, and then in a bit Leah came up to the front to tell us that Matt had dozed off on the couch and she covered him with a blanket.

Tricia said, "Good. You can drive some more."

I said no to that because Leah had been driving for two straight days, and she, too, was tired.

I said, "Just find a hotel and we'll stop."

But Tricia was angry, and we knew it. We found a Holiday Inn and stopped. I, once again, rented two rooms, but Paddy said he would stay in the RV with Tallahassee, the dog. I said we did not expect Paddy to dog-sit for us, but he insisted. In the morning, he said both he and Tallahassee slept well. He even took her outside on the grass before we all came into the RV to head for breakfast. As I said before, Paddy Hyndman was the best friend ever, and I hoped he knew how much we loved him.

We entered Texas, and I counted the states. Three more to California. But Texas was a big one, and it would probably take a day and a half to travel across the entire state.

We kept on going along the I-10. Thankfully, our drive was uneventful. I kept bothering Matt and asking if he felt all right. I was very worried about his stomach, but he was eating well, drinking plenty of fluids, and was going to the bathroom normally. I knew this because I was one of three women who were helping him. Matt said he felt fine, but he was very quiet and tired easily. I still worried about everything.

Nearing Arizona, I realized Matt was acting strangely. He was very quiet but when questioned, would snap at me. He was argumentative, extremely crabby, and somewhat agitated. We stopped at a rest stop near Phoenix, and I expressed my concern to Leah and Tricia. Leah had no comment, but Tricia did. She said since she was the person dispensing Matt's medications, she and Matt decided he no longer needed his Zoloft for depression, so she stopped it. I hit the ceiling. The three of us girls got into an argument in the parking lot. Matt and Paddy did not want to be involved, so they quickly returned to the RV to wait for us.

Tricia told me Matt no longer needed his Zoloft, and since he's an adult, he has the right to make his own decisions. I said that "adult" cannot even scratch his own head or eat his own sandwich or go to the bathroom by himself, so he is in no position to make his own medical decisions. Besides, having been married to a very busy and savvy internist for over twenty-five years, I knew that you did not discontinue antidepressants all at once but gradually decreased them. What Matt was exhibiting were withdrawal symptoms. Thank goodness we were only about ten hours from home, maybe less if traffic was light.

After our argument, we all climbed into the RV and drove on. A few minutes later, Leah received a phone call from Shayna, who was at home and making preparations for Matt's arrival. Another friend of Matt and Leah's was helping Shayna set up a food table and make a "Welcome Home" banner for Matt, but they heard from Tricia to cancel all activities. I had no idea what was happening. Leah and Shayna had planned a little coming-home party for Matt with a few of his friends and some of Jeremy's and my friends. Some of them had known Matt all his life, and most of them were very anxious to see him. And now they had been told not to come. I asked Matt why he would be reluctant to see his friends, but he just stared at me. I called Jeremy when we crossed into Los Angeles County and said we would be home within the hour. I was so excited. I was finally coming home, and it felt wonderful. What was even more special was the guy sitting in the back of the RV. Matt was anxiously waiting for the transfer onto the I-34, where we would exit onto Riverside Drive and turn onto our street.

Jeremy and Shayna were waiting by the front curb and were both waving excitedly. Leah had a little trouble parking the RV on our narrow street, so we had to go around the block and park on the other side. Matt jumped out of the RV and into his dad's and sister's arms. The three of them were hugging, crying, and holding on to each other.

Leah, Tricia, Paddy, and I busied ourselves with unloading the RV. Jeremy helped us while Shayna took Matt into the house. We decided to finish unpacking in the morning because we were all extremely tired.

Matt and Shayna were sitting closely on the couch, and Shayna was scratching Matt's head. Since scalp skin had been used for Matt's new eyelids, he was always complaining of profuse itching.

He would say to me, "Mom, please bring those French tips over here and scratch my head!"

And then, "Scratch harder! I'm so itchy!"

I was afraid of tearing the fragile new skin, so I would always scratch or rub his head gently, but he wanted my French tips to dig into his scalp. We tried to take it easy that night.

We had a tremendous amount of food on our dining room table, and I wondered how we could possibly eat all of it. We were expecting friends, but no one was there. As I was packing up the leftovers and putting salads into Tupperware bowls, I asked Tricia how our little party had fallen apart. She seemed to imply that she talked Matt out of it, and he was so easily swayed he went along with it. For the second time that day, I hit the ceiling. I seemed to be sweating all the small things. I know Matt was looking forward to seeing his friends and Jeremy's and my friends who would have been there, but that did not happen. I told Tricia that when Matt was in the hospital, a bunch of her girlfriends came to support her. I felt I had been very gracious and let all of them into Matt's room even though I knew they and Matt had never met. I thought it was insensitive to keep Matt's friends away from him now that we were home. I was wondering if I had made a mistake by bringing Tricia back to California with us. After all, she was not Matt's wife, and Jeremy and I were not about to relinquish taking care of Matt. I made the agreement with myself to stand by my decisions about Matt's well-being and medical care until she walked down the aisle with him and not a second sooner.

We were all very tired, and every bone in my body ached after our long drive, so I was eager for bed. I quickly unpacked my suitcase, and Jeremy inflated the bed-in-a-minute for Paddy. We brushed Matt's teeth, gently washed his face, put his pajamas on, and tucked him into bed. For the first time in a long time, I slept very peacefully, and when the alarm rang at six thirty in the morning, I was eager to start my day in my own house. I was anxious for a cup of Jeremy's cappuccino, and I wanted to sit on the patio with him and sip my coffee and just be with my husband for a few minutes before he would start to prepare for his busy day in the office.

We never got the chance to sit on the patio because my cell phone was ringing. I answered it, and it was "Mama Wanda." That was Matt's name for Tricia's mom, Wanda She asked if we were watching TV. I said it was only 6:30 a.m. and the TV was not on yet. She said to hurry and put it on because there had been a plane crash in New York City and the plane had hit the Empire State Building. Of course that was not quite accurate because when we turned the TV on, Matt Lauer and Katie Couric were reporting on the plane that hit the Twin Towers of the Trade Center, and it looked like an act of terrorism. For the entire day, Matt, Tricia, Paddy, and I watched TV.

We watched in horror as the Towers collapsed, and I remember Matt saying, "My god, there might be people in those buildings! Hopefully everyone got out safely."

Tuesday, September 11, 2001, was a horrible day for our country, but we were home. I felt so lucky to have arrived safely the night before. And I felt so sorry for all those poor people in New York.

Shayna had classes that day at Moorpark College, and Leah had to get back to her job in San Diego, so my girls were both out the door by 9:00 a.m. I had missed the two of them tremendously, and I wished they could both stay home for the morning, but responsibilities took them their separate ways.

Paddy was hoping to get back to Daytona Beach that week, but with the turmoil in the country, all flights were cancelled and LAX was practically shut down. Paddy ended up staying with us for about ten days. We enjoyed having him, and he was great with Matt. Paddy has a great sense of humor, so there was a lot of laughter in our home. I think all of us was feeling better.

Finally the following Friday, Paddy was able to get a flight to Daytona Beach. He, too, had responsibilities at Phil Air, and his students were waiting for him.

We took Paddy to LAX, but we were not allowed to take him to the main terminal. Things had changed at the airport, and we had to drop him off in a parking lot, where he boarded a bus that took him to the airline gate. We hugged him and thanked him for helping us and for just being our dear friend, and he was on his way. Before boarding the bus, he and Matt hugged, and both of them started to cry.

Matt said, "I love you, man."

And Paddy said, "Take care of yourself, my friend. I love you, too. Get better soon."

We hated to see that fellow leave because another part of Florida was behind us, but it was a very happy part that was dear to our hearts.

In a few days Tricia was called back to work, so once again, we made the trip to LAX, where we left her off in the parking lot. She would return in about five days.

Since Jeremy went to work and Shayna had classes every day, Matt and I were left alone in the house. I had Matt all to myself and cherished every moment that I had with him. Matt especially loved to talk about his plans for the future, but I noticed he always became sad during our conversations, because at that point his future was very uncertain.

During our first few days alone, Jeremy called with a phone number of a Dr. Peter Grossman, who was at the Grossman Burn Center in Sherman Oaks. Jeremy had spoken to Dr. Grossman, and he would be taking over Matt's care now that we were home. I had to call for an appointment as soon as possible.

Our appointment was set for the following Monday. I drove Matt to Dr. Grossman's office, and Jeremy met us there. The three of us discussed a game plan for Matt's treatment, and we would begin as soon as possible. Matt seemed to be very complacent and agreed to the plan Dr. Grossman proposed.

The following week I took Matt to the hospital where the first surgery would be "releases" under Matt's arms. A chunk of skin would be taken from his hip and placed under the arm, giving Matt the ability to raise his arms above his head. That being done, Matt recovered very well. The biggest problem was his hip. He was unable to roll over in bed, and he was in a lot of pain. I gave him pain pills around the clock for a few days until the pain subsided. Jeremy and

I felt it was unnecessary to suffer when there were medications that could help.

After the surgery, I would exercise Matt's arms so he would remain limber. We found that everyday living and moving around kept Matt's arms loose, and he started to look less rigid. He also said he was feeling better, which warmed my heart.

On Friday afternoon, Matt followed me into the kitchen and said, "Mom, I need to go shopping."

I said, "What do you need?"

He said he wanted to buy Tricia an engagement ring and he wanted to do it soon.

The next day Jeremy and I took him downtown to the Jewelry Mart to look at rings. Jeremy had a patient who was in the jewelry business and told us to look him up if we were ever shopping or needed a gift. We had to push Matt in his wheelchair. He wanted to walk, but he was too weak to walk the distance from the parking lot to the building, and there were so many people I was afraid Matt would get knocked over.

He was eye level with the counter and was looking at the engagement rings when he said, "They don't have what I'm looking for!"

We had no idea what he was shopping for, so he described the ring to the jeweler. Tricia had told Matt exactly what she wanted. They did not have that style, so it would have to be custom made, but that was what Tricia ordered, and Matt wanted to get her exactly what she wanted. As Matt and Jeremy were negotiating prices with the jeweler, it occurred to me that Matt had no money to pay for this ring so Jeremy and I would be paying. After that had been taken care of, the jeweler told us the ring would be ready in three days so we could pick it up at his house Tuesday evening.

A couple of day later, Jeremy, Matt, and I picked up the ring, and Matt was very satisfied. It was a gorgeous one-carat diamond in the center with two half-carat diamonds on either side in a platinum setting. It was exquisite, and we all liked it. Matt gave it to me to hide until he decided to give it to Tricia.

The next morning, Mama Wanda called and wanted to speak to Matt. Because he could not hold the phone to his ear, I would put him on speaker, and he would lie in bed and be able to talk. I walked out of the room, but I could hear bits and pieces of his conversation.

Wanda said, "I hear you're planning something important with my daughter, you piece of shit!"

Matt was silent. What I wanted to do was run into the room, grab the phone, and tell Wanda the conversation was over. And when she had something nice to say she could call back, but until then there would be no reason to call. Of course I never said anything, but I was quite angry. We had taken Tricia in and treated her like another daughter. Whenever I went to Nordstrom and bought something for my girls, I bought the same thing for her. I was very happy for Matt that he and Tricia were together, but I was starting to wonder if this was the best thing for him.

The next day, Matt and I drove to the FlyAway Bus Terminal in Van Nuys, where we picked up Tricia, who was home from her workweek. Matt wanted to stop at an outdoor hamburger stand for lunch, so we found a table in the shade and had a quick bite to eat. Tricia said she spoke to her mother, who said she had had a conversation with Matt. I have no idea what Mom told Tricia, but when I said her mom had called Matt a piece of shit which had upset me tremendously, Tricia nastily said, "My mother didn't say that!"

Okay, I guess I was hearing things.

Matt said very quietly, "Yes, she did."

Everyone was quiet after that, and we rode home in silence.

I felt that something was happening in my house, but frankly, I had no idea what it was, and if I did, I did not know what to do about it. Shayna was now eighteen years old, had graduated from high school, and was busy dating a number of young men who would come to our house to pick her up. One evening in late September, a young man named Alex arrived to take Shayna to the movies. They would stop and pick up Shayna's friend Alexis, and she would have a blind date with Alexis's friend.

Jeremy and I were reading in our room about midnight when we heard the key in the front door. Shayna and Alexis were home, and they were looking for something in the refrigerator. Jeremy remarked that the guys must not have offered the girls any food if they were scrounging around the cupboards after a date.

Suddenly Shayna ran into our room with the door hitting the wall and said to me, "Mom, am I gay?"

I said, "I don't know, Shayna. That's something you have to decide about yourself."

She said, "Well, Tricia said I'm having disastrous dates because I'm gay and haven't admitted it yet!"

I had no idea what to say, nor did Jeremy. We told Shayna we would love her no matter if she were gay or straight, but she was devastated. She told me the next day that she had never thought about being gay, but now that Tricia had planted that seed, she was not sure of her sexuality. This was an ongoing sore point around our house, with Jeremy, Leah, and I trying to comfort Shayna. I believe Leah confronted Tricia on behalf of her sister and told her to not get involved in family matters. After all, she was not family—yet.

Shayna kept obsessing about her sexuality, and I continued to tell her it did not matter. She would figure it out at some point. I thought about that beautiful diamond ring hidden in my bedroom closet!

For the rest of 2001, we made frequent trips to Dr. Grossman's office for assessment. Our next step was a surgery where Dr. Grossman would inject Matt all over his body with steroid shorts to alleviate the itching. That proved to be such a big help to Matt.

The nurse also told us that there was a burn survivor support group that met once a month in the hospital and maybe we would like to join. Matt thought that would be a good idea, but Tricia said absolutely not! He did not need to air his dirty laundry to a bunch of strangers. I was surprised that she felt that way, but Matt and I were excited to join and meet everyone. We went to our first meeting the following Wednesday and were delighted to meet Brad and Lianne and Jesse and Bill and Sue and Yolanda and a bunch of others who would have a big effect on Matt and me. Listening to all their stories put things in perspective for us. We realized that our journey would not be traveled alone. Every one of those folks were waiting to listen to our story and comfort us when we talked about our fears, our concern of our worries about recovery. On our second meeting, Jesse said, "I think I'll get a cup of coffee," and Brad retorted, "Don't burn yourself!" Matt and I just sat there, but everyone else laughed.

Brad told us that one day, when we least expected it, we would laugh again.

That day of laughter come about a month later when we were in a maxillofacial doctor's office at UCLA, Matt was ready for his prosthetic ears, so we contacted the dentist at the dental school, and off we went. I took a photo of Matt so the doctor could see the ears and what they looked like, but when he pushed my hair back, he said, "I don't need this photo anymore. He has your ears, so I know what to make." On our fourth visit, the ears were ready for Matt's first fitting. I had no idea they would be held firm by a glue of some sort.

"Wow," I said to Matt, "they look great!' He wanted the mirror to see, but the doctor said, "Hold your horses! I'm not done!"

I held the mirror for Matt, and he looked at his new ears very carefully. He gave his approval to the doctor, who did not seem impressed, and then the doctor walked out of the room to let the glue dry. While drying, Matt kept complaining that his right ear was itching profusely. I tried to help, but Matt wanted to scratch on his own. Well, the ear fell off and fell downward on the tile floor! It was stuck like glue, as they say! I couldn't get the ear pried off the floor. The doctor walked in, and oh, was he angry at us! While Matt and I were giggling, the doctor was reprimanding us for not appreciating his artwork and being so cavalier about a ruined silicone ear. He took the other ear off, put it in a ziplock bag, and handed it to me along with a tube of glue. He said, "You will get the repaired ear in the mail in about a week or so." We assumed we had been dismissed, so we left for home.

At our next burn survivor meeting, we told our story about the ear to our new friends, and everyone was nodding their heads and laughing with us. Matt looked at me, and I think we were reading each other's thoughts. We talked about it on our drive home, and Matt said we had learned a valuable lesson tonight. First, it's okay to laugh at stupid stuff; two, we were learning that our friends in the group would support us no matter what; and three, we're still us! That was the most important to us because on our arrival at home from the hospital, no one in our family knew who they were. Surrounded by all the emotional angst, we were all trying to get back to some sort of normal. "We're still us!" was a home run for us, and from that night, Matt and I knew we were on the road to recovery.

There next day Matt's friend Yoav stopped at our house in the morning. He wanted to show us his new car, a bright yellow Dodge Viper. All I could say was, "Wow!" They climbed into the car, I fastened Matt's seat belt, and they were off. Matt walked into the house about a half hour later looking wind-blown and happy. He loves cars almost as much as planes, and the short ride had done wonders for his psyche that day.

Spending time with Matt while Tricia was at work was what I loved best. Our times together were not easy or laid back, but involved a lot of hard work and effort, and quite often Matt and I would get into an argument. He hated having his mouth exercised because it was so uncomfortable. We did the mouth exercise faithfully every day Matt knew they were essential because the skin around his mouth was getting tighter, and he could not open his mouth wide enough to eat a hamburger. Dr. Grossman said our next step was "releasing" Matt's mouth. Some sort of slits would be made on each side of Matt's mouth so he could open wider. Surgery would be coming up soon, and we were all excited. Being excited for a surgery probably seems strange, but every one of these reconstructive surgeries was a step closer to normality. We were also going to Louisville, Kentucky, where Matt would have hand surgery. Before we arrived at the Jewish Hand Hospital, we had no idea which hand the surgeon would work on, or even what his plans were for reconstructive surgery.

The next morning we met the team, which consisted of the doctor, a very famous hand surgeon, the anaesthesiologist, two or three hand surgery nurses, and a few technicians. Next they showed us slides and explained how the doctor would sew Matt's arm to his forehead, hoping to create a blood supply once and for all. Once there was a blood supply in the arm, reconstructive surgery could begin. Matt and I discussed, at great length, the long road ahead. Tricia, who was with us at this time, said, "Why are you two being so negative and talking about how bad might be and how long it might take?"

Matt said, "Not being negative, just being realistic! The doctor told us the right hand and arm were useless and would most likely need to be amputated."

That was extremely hard to hear; Matt started to cry, and I felt sick, but we had an operation to get through, so we had to think about that.

We arrived at the surgery center bright and early next morning, and Matt immediately was taken back to the prep area to get ready. I was told someone would come and get me soon. I would be allowed to see Matt off to surgery. Because Matt's arm was badly injured, the nurses were unable to start an IV on him. They were kind enough to tell him they would do mask induction on him, and when he was asleep, one of them would start the IV in his foot. Matt liked the idea and was thanking everyone profusely. This time as he was wheeled to the operating room, he asked, "Will you be here when I wake up?"

I said, "Of course!" I told him how much I love him, and he said, "I love you, Ma!" and then he was gone. I felt that familiar feeling in my stomach, and I thought I might get sick.

I walked to the waiting area by myself and sat down with my book. Once again I found myself alone in a big room with lots of bulky couches and chairs. Tricia had gone back to work in the morning, so that left Matt and me to fend for ourselves.

Surgery took about five hours; after endless cups of tea, I was escorted back to the recovery room. Matt would be in the room for about an hour and then he would be discharged. We would go across the street to the Sheraton, where patients and their family could stay while undergoing hand procedures. There was a shuttle that took us to the hotel, and thankfully the driver helped me hoist Matt up to the stairs and into a seat. Once again we were getting stares. Matt's left forearm was attached to his head. He was a mess, as he said, and he would have to stay that way for ten days. Thankfully, there was a decent restaurant at the hotel, so I would go down there to buy food and bring it back up to the room. I knew it would be a long ten days. The hotel staff were so kind to us. One morning a maintenance man and our cleaning lady brought me a stationary bike and set it so that I could get some exercise. I was so grateful to be moving a bit!

After seven days of great discomfort to Matt since his arm was up in the air, I began to smell something putrid. I checked under the bed to see if we had dropped a piece of food, but found nothing. The smell seemed to be coming from Matt. Now I was worried about an infection. I called the hospital and was told to bring Matt in the next morning. There was a clinic for rechecks, and they would fit him in between the other patient. Once again I found myself in the waiting room. I was told that Matt had an infection in his arm, which was due to bacteria collecting on his arm and his forehead. The doctor would "take down" the arm from his head, it would be cleansed with an antibacterial rinse, we would be given a prescription for an oral antibiotic, and we would be on our way. That night Leah knocked on our hotel room door! Once again she would accompany us home. Tricia had taken an extra work so we would not be seeing her for another work or so.

The next morning after breakfast in the restaurant, I went to the hotel lobby to check out. The young lady at the desk had made cookies for Matt which she said could be a snack in the car. Our ride home was long and tedious, but Matt, Leah, and I always found something to talk about. As usual, Matt talked about his fear, what would become of his life, what occupation he could have. At twenty-four, he was so worried about being a loser. I began to spew out my mantra. His body had taken a beating, but he had a good brain. It would be his job to figure out how to put it to good use. He answered with an uncertain, "Hmm…"

Leah was able to stay with us for a couple of days, and Tricia came back from work so we were all together at home again. Matt said he wanted Chinese food for dinner that night from his favorite restaurant near our house.

Tricia said, "Well, I had Chinese food last night so I don't want that!" We just looked at each other. Matt explained that there were five people who did not have Chinese food last night, and that's what we all wanted. She said okay and enjoyed dinner as much as we did.

The next day I wanted to go to the mall to buy a gift, but Tricia said she wanted to go for a run, so Matt and I went together. While passing a counter in Macy's, Matt said, "Hey, Ma, look at this!" Chess set? He said we needed a chess set! Okay. We purchased a chess set and went home. We set it up on the coffee table in the family room, and then Matt said, "Sit down, Ma, let's play!" I guess he had forgotten I would have to be taught! Yes, he became my teacher. After about a week, we were playing chess. I was certainly not a good player, and I never won, but Matt loved chess so we played the game mostly every afternoon.

One afternoon, Matt said it was time he gave Tricia an engagement ring. What could we do to surprise her? We settled on dinner at a French restaurant in Burbank. Tricia told us her friend was coming to visit the following week so we would wait for her to be included in festivities. Now, how strange is it for her guy's family to go for dinner with the couple when a marriage proposal is planned for the evening? Jeremy and I did not want to go, but Matt insisted, saying he would not be able to get the ring out on his pocket, and what if the ring fell in the floor? He wanted help. So we all went. Matt regaled us with stories about Tricia and how they acquired their Shih-Tzu, Tallahassee. At his nod, Jeremy took the ring out of his pocket and put it under Tricia's nose. She was surprised, and she loved the ring. So now, my eldest was engaged! It was an exciting time, and there were well-wishers everywhere!

The next time Tricia went back to work, Matt had a surprise for me. "Mom," he said, "do you want to go for a ride?"

"Yeah sure," I said. He really wanted to drive, so we went out to the driveway, where his little Acura Integra was parked. I started it, and since it was a stick shift, he used the palm of his right hand to shift into reverse, and we went up and down the driveway for about an hour. I was exhausted, and Matt needed a nap. I promised him we would drive again tomorrow.

Tomorrow rolled around, and Matt said, "Is it time for our ride?" This day we ventured around the block. We lived in a very quiet neighbourhood where there was hardly any traffic, so I felt we were safe. Matt did superbly.

I remember back at Shands one of the hand surgeons had walked into the cafeteria where I was having a cup of coffee and said, "How's Matt today?"

I said he was resting comfortably.

She continued, "You know he'll never be able to drive a car or fly a plane again. In fact, I'm not sure what he'll ever be able to do again!"

Thank you, Doctor! I thought facetiously.

As we were going in circles around the block, I was hoping Matt would prove her wrong. I saw the silly grin on my son's face and the determination he had suddenly acquired, and I knew he would drive again.

About a week later, Matt had an appointment with Dr. Grossman. I decided to let him drive to the doctor's office! Oh, the screaming that came from him. I had never seen him so excited. We got into the car. I buckled his seat belt and started the car. He eased out of the driveway gently, and I saw him look both ways. I was so grateful that Dr. Grossman had "released" Matt's stiff neck and he was able to turn both ways. We turned left on to Riverside Drive and drove about a mile to get on to the I-134. He was so careful, and, oh, I was so nervous. Once again my son had my life in his hands, but my very competent, squeaky clean Matt was doing just fine. We arrived at Dr. Grossman's office, and Matt ran up to the reception-ist's desk to tell the ladies how he drove. They were so excited for him. Hugs and hoots of laughter become very normal for us. Dr. Grossman heard the good news and was congratulating Matt. We had just started a new chapter of life!

CHAPTER
THIRTEEN

Matt had a few more surgeries, most of them reconstructive, on his eyelids and mouth. He was now wearing a silicone mask about twenty-three hours per day. It was molded to his face and would cut down on swelling and scars. He said once he got accustomed to it, his face felt better and less itchy. Looking back, I'm glad we were so compliant. Despite the severity of his injury, his face looks quite good.

He was not wearing ears too often because the glue was extremely abrasive, and truthfully, he looked like Howdy Doody in those ears. Oh, how we loved to laugh about that. Matt decided to not go back to the UCLA dental school for new ones since we were going back and forth to Louisville, Kentucky, for hand surgeries at the Jewish hand hospital. We would travel out there nine times for surgeries. We had a conference with the doctor, and we agreed; the left arm and hand had not gotten any better despite ten surgeries. We were so disappointed, but what could we do? Matt tried to figure out what he could do with his life. He was engaged now and wanted to support his wife and a family.

Jeremy and I were so elated to have our son. We decided to give a party to honor Matt and Tricia. It would be held on Saturday,

March 16, 2002, exactly one year after Matt's accident. Tricia was very excited about an engagement party and was shopping for a new dress with her friend. I had a never-worn sparkly dress in the closet so there was no shopping for me.

RSVPs were arriving, and a banquet room had been rented at our favourite restaurant. I knew that Tricia was very excited about an engagement party, but all our family and friends came to see Matt and honor him and celebrate with him. There were lots of testimonials about Matt's resilience and strength. There were stories of flights with Matt in Southern California and going to restaurants for lunch or dinner and then flying back to Van Nuys Airport. They all ended their spiel with good wishes and much luck for Matt and Tricia. Matt was in tears, his sister was crying. Jeremy and I were emotional, and all our friends were teary eyed. Jeremy and I noticed that Tricia and her friends were talking to each other. They were ignoring everyone who was speaking. I assume we had somehow insulted them, I can't say, because I never saw the friends again. They all got into the limousine, and a friend of ours took them to their hotel. I was upset about this, but Jeremy said to ignore it all. I did, and it seemed to blow over.

We had a very busy summer of 2002. Weddings seemed to be prevalent. Surgeries were taking place, also. We traveled to Louisville, Kentucky, for two surgeries, and Dr. Grossman did two more surgeries on Matt. He reconstructed Matt's eyelids again and his mouth once more.

At the very end of 2002, Matt said he thought he was somewhat bored and felt he should be doing something constructive. He said to me, "I think I should go back to school and get my degree." Such music to my ears! He continued, "I've found a university where I can finish my degree online, and the new semester starts on January 6, about three weeks away."

During that summer, Jeremy also said he has a new job opportunity, and maybe we should check it out. I certainly had no desire to relocate, but it wasn't about me. Jeremy thought it might be nice to downsize our busy lifestyle, so we flew out to Oklahoma City to check it out and meet a few of the people Jeremy would be working with. The hospital was located in a small city called Edmond, which is a suburb straight north of Oklahoma City. It was a very nice city, and the houses were very nice, but we had a lot to talk about.

Matt and I were going back to Louisville for more surgery the following week, so I was not able to make decision about relocating. To me that was a big deal.

Our trip to Louisville, Kentucky, was uneventful. The doctor made some slits in between the fingers on Matt's left hand, but the surgery was not successful. He had hoped Matt would get some movement in his fingers, but that never happened. We drove home in silence.

After celebrating Thanksgiving and Hanukkah with our family, the New Year rolled around quickly.

January 6, 2003, stands out in my mind and not in a very good or positive way.

I was in my room, preparing for the day, when Tricia knocked on the door and walked in. She looked angry. She said, "I'm leaving!" I thought she meant she was going back to work, but she continued, "I just can't be with Matt anymore! I've had it!" She said, "We got into an argument and I threw the ring at him!" She said she was going to Salt Lake City to live with her friend, Lisa. And, oh, she said as she picked up Tal, the Shih Tzu, "You can have the dog! She really loves you and Matt, and she'll be happier with you!"

Matt was busy at the computer and signing up for classes. This semester was starting, and he was very excited. He never looked at Tricia as she was carrying her belongings to her car, and when she was finished, she walked out and slammed the door. The house shook, and still Matt didn't look up or say everything to her.

Jeremy and I took Matt out for dinner that night. Obviously, we ended up at our favourite Chinese restaurant in Burbank. We talked about the breakup and his classes and what he would be taking. He had registered, and his classes at 8:00 a.m. the next day would include crew resource management, and he had declared his major as aviation/private pilot. We, of course, asked about all his classes, and he said his books would be arriving in a few days. It was so wonderful to see him exited. We asked him about Tricia and what happened, but he was evasive so we let it go. I hated the thought of Matt starting a new project with a broken heart, but when we asked again about her departure, he said, "I'm rather relieved!" We never brought it up again, and, interestingly, his relationship with his sisters improved. He continued to study every day, he refused going out for dinner because he had to read, and he was doing wonderfully.

Jeremy's mantra has always been, "There are two sides to every story!" We are sure Matt contributed to the demise of his relationship with Tricia, but it was really none of our business, so we never asked.

We had also decided to take the plunge and move to Edmond, Oklahoma, and the big day would be around the end of February.

Leah decided to give us a going-away cocktail party at a private room she had rented at a restaurant in Encino, California. We never really know how many people she invited, but we had a packed house—all our friends from the hospital where Jeremy practiced, all my friends from years of car pools, all Matt's friends from the burn support group, and some of our temple friends. We had a great cocktail party, and lots of wine was drunk. It was a time for more speeches. All of Jeremy's and my friends remembered our thirty years as friends from UCLA internships, residencies, and fellowships and then on to private practice. My friends recalled all our driving expeditions to classes, on field trips, to the local store for a snack before dropping off everyone at the ice rink. We had so much history under our belts. I really did not want to leave Southern California, but Jeremy assured me it would be a good move.

FOURTEEN

A huge green-and-yellow moving van pulled up to our house on a Tuesday morning. Jeremy and I were ready and dressed, and the three movers came inside.

I helped Matt get dressed and then he and I took a walk to Starbucks to get everyone coffee and Danishes. Matt and I had our snack inside because it was two less cups to carry and two less dough-nuts in the bag. As we were sitting at our table, a limousine parked outside right in front of us and a man in a suit walked straight toward us. It was John Ritter. He asked Matt how he was doing and then he asked, "How many operations have you had?"

Matt said, "About forty."

He said, "Holy smoke! Hang in there, young man! And nice to meet you!" When we got home with our treats, we told every-one what had happened, they loved the story, and then it was back to moving all our furniture on to the truck. That took all day, but finally around midnight, they packed Jeremy's car on to the truck and closed it shut.

Jeremy packed up Matt's computer, his screen, his books, and we put it in the RV we were renting. I had picked up Leah at the

Burbank airport earlier that afternoon so she and Matt could drive my Lexus to Oklahoma City. We stayed in a hotel that night, and early in the morning, we got on to the 134 and headed to the I-40, which would take us right into Oklahoma. Matt and Leah were in my car, and Jeremy and I were in the RV with our dogs: Sally the Golden, Molly our black lab, Marty our yellow lab boxer lunatic, and Tallahassee, the Shih Tzu. We also had all Matt's school supplies and all my plants.

Matt and Leah were behind us and keeping up with us. We drove for about five hours and decided to stop in Flagstaff for dinner and maybe get a room for the night. We settled on the Hilton, and Jeremy and Matt took the dogs for a walk and put them back in the RV. Fortunately it was a warm evening, so the fur kids had their pillows and blankets to sleep with and they would be fine. At 3:00 a.m., Jeremy went back outside again. He gave each of them a Milk-Bone biscuit, and they went back to sleep.

After our free breakfast of yogurt and coffee, we were back in our vehicle and on the I-40. It would be a straight ride east into Oklahoma City. At the border of Arizona and New Mexico, we found a very cool rest area that had a fenced-in area for pets. Since there was no one else, there we took the leashes off our dogs and let them run. Jeremy got a couple of their balls from the RV, and we played with them for a while. Even our little Tal got in on all the action, but with her short, stubby legs, the poor girl did not catch any balls!

We got into the RV, and Matt and Leah got into the car. Instead of driving away, Matt came up to the windows on his dad's side and said, "Dad, my hand hurts!"

Oh no, I thought.

Jeremy checked Matt's hand, and sure enough, the top of his left hand was a little bit swollen and starting to get red. It was also a bit warm to the touch. What kind of infection could he be getting? Jeremy gave him an antibiotic that he had in his bag, and we gave him Tylenol and he went back to the car. We were finally on our way.

We noticed that the temperature was dropping, and we needed more heat in the RV. At the next rest stop, it must have been thirty degrees colder than earlier that morning When we let the dogs out again to run around, we all needed our jackets. Matt said his hand had stopped throbbing. We were watching our dogs running around, and we were watching snowflakes flying around, which did not make me happy.

The I-40 was getting more treacherous and icy the further east we drove. We stopped at a truck stop because we saw our moving truck parked there. We got out of the RV and went to the big truck where our three movers were drinking coffee. We discussed the weather, and they said it might be better if we stopped for the night. We were near Albuquerque, and we found a pet--friendly hotel, so we stopped and traipsed into our rooms with three Labs and a Shih Tzu. What a bunch we were!

Thankfully, the next morning brought lots of the sunshine, but it was only 25 degrees. Of course the dogs wanted to run around before breakfast, but, truthfully, my toes were freezing!

Once again we met up with the movers at a truck stop along the I-40. We brought coffee, and when we come back to the RV, we were locked out! The Labs were all sleeping, but Tal, who was jumping from window to window, must have stepped on the lock button inside, which locked all doors. We stood there laughing, but what should we do? We needed to get into the RV. Tal was agitated, and it looked like she was about to cry. She wanted access to her family.

Todd, one of the movers had found a piece of wire near a dumpster and was able to unlock the door for us. We were so impressed, because who, after all, knows how to do that?

Road condition were icy along the I-40, and everyone was driving slowly. It took another day and a half to get to Oklahoma City, where it was cold and rainy, but at least hot snowing. We were able to get adjoining rooms at the Days Inn, where we left our dogs with their pillows and blankets, and we headed out for dinner and then to meet our realtor and get the keys to our new house. We brought Matt and Leah to show them the house, and Matt had a good time choosing his room. He chose the room at the back of the house which had a bathroom attached and another room on the other side. Matt declared that would be his "office."

The next morning was moving day. We stopped at Denny's for a quick breakfast and then went to our new house. We let our dogs into our huge fenced-in backyard, where Sally, our golden, promptly dove into the pool for a swim. We did not have access to any towels, so the poor girl had to air dry and she was not happy.

The first thing the movers brought in was the kitchen table and chairs, so Jeremy brought Matt's computer and books in from the RV and set him up at the table so he could do his schoolwork. I still can't figure out how he managed to ignore all the activity going on around him and keep on studying.

Of course it was pizza night in our house. We, along with the three movers, gathered around the table and had a fun dinner. As soon as we finished, Matt went back to studying.

It was close to midnight when Jeremy's car came off the truck and went into the garage Boxes were everywhere, but we prepared our beds and went to sleep anyway.

In the morning I got out of bed and opened our bedroom shutter. I may have screamed, but I'm not sure. Covering the ground was a blanket of snow. I think I started to cry. I was so upset. I told my husband that I had not signed up for a climate with snow, so let's call the movers back and go home to Southern California. We were slipping and sliding in the driveway because it was so icy, and we were taking Leah to the airport so she could get back to work on Monday.

Matt was still complaining that his left hand was itching, and it was redder and more swollen than a day or so ago. Jeremy said he would look for a local hand specialist on Monday. I hoped we didn't have to make a trip back to Louisville.

We dug into the boxes and got all our clothes unpacked and arranged our dresser drawers, and I was working in the kitchen. We did find an Olive Garden close by us. We brought food home for dinner, and shortly after that our doorbell rang. Our first visitor in Edmond! It turned out to be Todd, one of our movers, who helped pack a family on the truck and get them on their way to Houston. He would be spending a few days with us and helping me unpack and set everything up.

Early Monday morning, Jeremy took Matt and his swollen hand to the doctor, and I stayed home with Todd. We unpacked books and photos, and he even hung a painting. We have a huge Lebedang that has always hung over our fireplace, so Todd hung it in our family room above the mantel. It looked spectacular, and I kept staring at it.

Matt and Jeremy returned at lunch time and did not have great news. A pin, which had been placed in his hand to spread his fingers apart, had somehow worked its way up to the top of his hand and was starting to poke through the skin, causing swelling, redness, and pain. It would have to be surgically removed.

We left for the hospital the next day at 5:30 a.m. It was a balmy 17 degrees and very windy. I'm ashamed to tell you. I was still pouting since I saw all that snow! We had to stop abruptly, but had no idea what was happening. Seems like a mama deer was crossing the road with her two babies following. I said to Jeremy, "Where do we live? What are we doing here?" I was really missing the hustle and bustle of the 134 and 405 in the Los Angeles.

Matt's surgery was very simple. He was barely asleep when the surgeon touched the hand and the pin came out on its own. More 7 UP and crackers and we were on our way home. Todd had been busy while we were at the hospital. He had done the entire garage and had nailed the peg board up and hung Jeremy's tools. It looked great, and we wouldn't have to do a thing to it or change anything. Jeremy was thrilled.

Matt continued to study all day, and Jeremy and Todd hoisted our big screen TV onto our new stand and hooked up our DVR system and the surround sound system. It was really beginning to feel like home, except for the snow and frigid temperatures.

I had also arranged my kitchen and dishes and silverware and pots and pans. I had made a quick trip to the grocery store that was close by so I would be able to make dinner. After a delicious meal of chicken, broccoli, and a green salad, Jeremy turned on the TV and Matt asked if I would proofread his first paper that he had written for his English composition class. He submitted it the next day and said he was glad this first paper was done. He had four more to go before the end of the semester.

At the end of the week, we took Todd to the bus station, where he would travel to Houston and meet up with his fellow movers and the truck. They were on their way to Daytona Beach, so we gave Todd money to get Matt's belongings from the POD storage and bring him his furniture on their trip back to Oklahoma City. We never heard from or saw Todd again.

A couple of months later, Matt and I flew to Daytona Beach, rented a U-Haul, and found a guy who loaded the U-Haul with Matt's bed, his couch, his desk, boxes of books, posters of sports cars and planes, and we were ready to drive back to Oklahoma City. First, we stopped at the Olive Garden and had dinner with Matt's friend Paddy and Robby, a flight student of Matt's. We ate lots of spaghetti, laughed a lot, and cried a bit. We were helped into the U-Haul, but not until there were more hugs. That was June of 2003. We have not seen Paddy since then, but heard he is flying in South Africa or somewhere, I'm not sure. He has gotten married and has one daughter. Matt has not heard a word from or about from Robby, his student.

Matt insisted on driving because he didn't think I was familiar with a truck. To my surprise, he was doing very well, and because I felt so safe with him in the driver's seat, I fell asleep. I awoke to my cell phone ringing and Jeremy asking me, "Where are you?"

"Chattanooga," I replied, "why?"

He explained the city was surrounded by tornadoes, and he was about to go into the inner closet with the dogs.

"Tornadoes?" I said as I turned to Matt. Oh, I know what tornadoes are, but didn't we just finish with snow and ice storm? Now, it seemed we would be facing another meteorologic phenomenon, and I just wanted to go back to Southern California. We got home late at night, and early Sunday morning, an acquaintance of ours came and unloaded the U-Haul, and we set up Matt's computer and his books in his "office." He would now be able to study in his "suite" and loved his privacy.

We also picked up all his jeans, khakis, and dress pants from an alteration person. We asked her to remove all zippers and sew in a Velcro "T" so Matt could undo his own pants. We were working on independence. It was taking us a while to get there, but we were doing it.

Matt would spend most of the day at his desk studying. He had learned to turn the pages of his book with a pencil using the eraser. I had to smile when I saw that, and I thought, *We are moving right along, world!*

On, or about, May 31, Matt joined his dad and me in the kitchen and said, "First semester is finished! All 4 As!"

Wow, we were so proud of Matt! He had put a tremendous amount of work into his studies, and it had paid off! He also said he would like to continue and go to summer school for two classes. His dad and I supported his decision. He said he would try to complete his aviation algebra class this summer, and he had a bright idea. He had taken another math class at Embry-Riddle University with a phenomenal teacher, and he would like to fly her out and have her be his personal tutor. We said okay to that also, but didn't know if it was doable. Matt called her that night, and she told him that she would be interested and was not teaching summer school at the university so she was totally available. First, she would call Utah Valley University and speak to the head of the math department to see if she could get permission to tutor Matt. They were familiar with his position, so they said yes. The only thing, they would grade his exam.

We arranged to pick Linda up to OKC airport in three days, and she and Matt would go straight to work. She loved our guest room and said that she might not leave after six weeks! We liked her immediately because she loved to talk with us and she loved Jeremy's barbequed chicken. We four ate together every night, and Linda would always help with the dishes and then we were off to bed.

On the morning of July 8, 2003, Matt and Linda were at the kitchen table earlier than the rest of us. It was one last review session before the exam at 9:00 a.m. Linda set Matt up at the computer in his room and came out to the kitchen. We decided to make Matt some chocolate chip cookies. The Labs were outside running around in the fenced-in yard, and Tal was in the kitchen with us sleeping.

Matt come out after about three hours and had submitted his exam to the math department. He heard back from them in about an hour. A solid A. He got everything right on the exam! Thank you, Linda! What a coup for them.

That night we roasted a big chicken and made salad and potatoes. I even opened a bottle of wine to celebrate the success of the first summer school session! Matt would not be attending the second session because we would be going back to Los Angeles for more reconstructive surgery. Dr. Grossman would do another graft on his mouth because his lower lip was jutting out and he constantly had chapped lips.

Our celebration dinner with Linda was a huge success, but then Linda said, "Say, Matt, how long are you gonna have your mom feed you? You just passed a very specialized math course, don't you think you should feed yourself?"

Silence at the table. We said good night, but I knew Linda had planted the seed and Matt would be thinking about her words.

In the morning I made oatmeal, and he was struggling to eat with his spoon. He made a mess, but he ate most of his cereal.

It was now on OKC Will Rogers, where Linda would catch her flight back to Daytona Beach.

CHAPTER
FIFTEEN

We headed for Los Angeles about a week later. Matt was doing all the driving now and enjoying every minute of it.

Dr. Grossman would be operating on Matt's mouth again, and once again Matt came from the operating room with a big green bolster on his lip, allowing him to only drink food from a straw. The next three days would consist of milk shakes and Cokes from a straw.

On our drive home back to Oklahoma, we stepped at McDonald's, and Matt had to settle for a regular cheeseburger because that's all he could open his mouth. He held his burger in a strange manner, basically with his two elbows, but he was eating it by himself. To eat his French fries, he spilled the bag on his burger wrapper and could bend down and pick up a fry with his tongue. It was working! He was eating by himself! It was not refined dining, but I noticed no one was looking at us and no one really cared!

The second full semester started as we arrived home from Los Angeles. Matt was back to studying all day and only came out of his office to eat.

Jeremy and a friend of ours had changed all the doorknobs in the house to handles. Matt could certainly not put his hand around a knob and twist, but he could pull down the handle and run out of the house in the case of an emergency.

I also thought I was ready to join a gym, so I joined our local Jazzercise facility close by and would go to aerobics classes about 3–4 times per week. I left comfortable knowing Matt could get out of the house if he had to, and I was only gone for about an hour and a half. I would quickly rush home to make sure he was all right and the dogs were all sleeping. I, too, was gaining some independence.

I always say that life as we knew it came to an end the day Matt had his accident. It was an event that no one planned for, and many parents receive that call that no mom or dad should ever get.

I was observing that little by little, we were building a new life for our family. Matt's self-esteem was soaring, presumably because he was doing so well at school. Another semester and four more As. The ear-to-ear smile on Matt's face as he told his dad and me the class results was priceless.

All was going smoothly at our house and then Yoav and Brian, Matt's two good friends, were going to fly out for a visit. By fly out, I mean they were going to rent a plane and fly to OKC. Yoav was a pilot, and Brian was a helicopter pilot. The visit was a huge success! The boys, who had been friends for many years, were so happy to see each other.

Yoav suggested, "How about a flight?" So Yoav, Matt, Brian, and Jeremy got into the car and off they went. A little added tidbit I learned, the plane they would be flying was all too familiar—a multi-engine Piper Seneca. The same plane that Matt had been flying when it crashed. Oh, I had to work really hard at calming down my heart. It would not be still! And it was a long three hours. When they got home, I made coffee, and I had some cookies in the freezer. The buzz at the kitchen table was planes, planes, and more planes. Matt was smiling like a total goofball.

The next morning when the guys left, Matt said to me, "Ma, there is something more I must do! Fly and get all my licenses back!"

I said, "If that's what you really must do, then go for it!" Truthfully, I had reservations about him flying again. After all, one crash in a lifetime is enough!

So now in between studying, Matt and I would go to Wiley Post Airport, where Matt would have a lesson. I would stand by large windows in the flight school and watch that single-engine plane take off! As usual I was in tears! I felt like I had taken a few steps back in progress. What was wrong with me?

Matt continued to study, take classes, and take flight lessons for the next year, and in the spring of 2005, school came to an end and Jeremy and I had a summa cum laude graduate of the Utah Valley University! We were so proud of our son. Looking at him and his battered body, I was shocked to see that Matt, his dad, and I were evolving somehow. We were becoming different people, but I wasn't able to put that into words yet.

CHAPTER
SIXTEEN

June of 2005 was an exciting time for us. Our oldest daughter was getting married, so we were busy planning a wedding. The festivities took place the last weekend of June, and Matt was delighted to be a groomsman.

After the excitement of a family wedding, Matt and I were on our way to Peoria, Illinois, to meet with the medical director of the FAA. We had all Matt's medical records from Shands Medical Center. It took Jeremy and me two entire evening to organize the records. Mixed in with Matt's records were some other poor guy's reports, so we took everything out and sent it back to medical records at the hospital. We never got any feedback, so I hope everything got there in a timely fashion.

Matt had a mini physical with the doctor there, and he said Matt was "as fit as a fiddle." He wanted Matt to continue taking flight lessons, and he said there was no reason why Matt couldn't earn back his private, instrument, commercial, flight instructor (CFI), flight instructor instruments (CFII) and multi-engine instructor (MEI). He said we should come back when that was accomplished.

"Wow, lots of work," I said.

Matt said, "Where am I going?"

Back to Oklahoma we went! Matt resumed lessons at the airport, and he even would drive himself there sometimes. I was in awe of Matt, but I didn't want the guy to get a big head!

We had graduated to a life of lots of laughter. That was so good for our recovery. We laughed about so many things, and we laughed about lots of the happenings in the hospital. We were recovered sufficiently to find humor instead of tears.

Flight lessons continued through the next year, and in the spring, we welcomed our first grandchild and Matt's first nephew. He was so excited. Unexpectedly, Leah and her husband and baby ended up moving to Edmond. Now we were city neighbours and thrilled about having more family so close by.

On a very cold, blustery day in February, we went to Wiley Post Airport to meet the FAA agent. Matt was scheduled to take his SODA flight (Statement of Demonstrated Ability). Once again, I found myself by those ceiling-to-floor windows along with Leah and the baby in the stroller. Joining us was a cameraman and a reporter from channel 4. We have no idea how they got there or who invited them. They also suggested we go outside where the lights would be better for filming. It was so cold outside. Leah and I had the hoods on our coats over our heads and had the baby wrapped up in the blankets. I heard the roar of a plane engine, and then suddenly there was that single-engine Piper Arrow taking off and going higher and higher. The wind was blowing, and the tears on my face were freezing. The cameraman was following the plane as it banked right and disappeared from our view. The reporter had questions for me about Matt and his plans for the future and in aviation. Now, since it had been such a windy day, my hair was dishevelled, my mascara smeared, and yet I stood there proudly and spoke about my son. That clip did appear on the 5:00 p.m. news.

In the FBO (fixed base operation), we all gathered around and listened to the FAA agent's word, "Pass!"

OMG, my very personal pilot! I was so proud! Matt had now earned back his private pilot license, instrument and commercial license, and after talking to his friend Yoav, he was off to LAX to look at a plane to buy. They spent a lot of time looking at planes and flying them in test rides. After a few weeks in Los Angeles, Matt settled on the Socata Trinidad TB20, which was manufactured in France. Jeremy flew out to LAX on Friday morning, and he would accompany Matt home in the plane. Matt had taken a bunch of lessons and had become certified in the Trinidad. His dad would be with him in the cockpit if another pair of hands was needed. They got as far as Amarillo, Texas, and called to say they would stay overnight since fog and poor visibility was coming in and we were getting an ice storm in Oklahoma City.

The next morning was sunny, and the temperature went up to 55 degrees. My boys called. They would be taking off in a few minutes, and I would pick them up at the Guthrie, Oklahoma, airport in about three hours.

I arrived ahead of them and parked and was able to see all the planes landing. I saw a beautiful low-winged plane that was white with tan markings, and I wondered if that was ours. Matt and Jeremy showed me the plane, and I ran my fingers across the hood. It felt so slick, and it smelled great!

Matt said to me, "Do you like it, Ma?"

I said, "Sure is beautiful!"

He said, "It's all ours, and we will go someplace soon!" I did look forward to a flight with Matt, but I would never push it since Matt was busy once again. He was looking for a career to settle into, so he was now at real estate school. He was eager to have a Monday-through-Friday job. I said that many jobs are not just Monday-Friday and are still traditional. But he said he had started the course and he would finish it. He did pass the state test, and he did get a job at a local real estate agency, and I got the impression he was really excited about his five-day-a-week job. He said that coming up that week there was a meeting that he would not be attending because he had no seniority so he would have the afternoon off.

I said, "I have a great idea, Matt! Take me for a flight!"

Little did I know that I'd be starting my education in weather! I had opened up a can of worms, but I did get my flight. I was taught how to contact flight service for a full weather briefing, and Matt taught me how to change the settings on the radio as Air Traffic Control gave them to us. That was a tough one for me because ATC spoke so fast I couldn't understand them. Matt would have to tell me the numbers and then I would turn the dials. Matt really needed help with that because he could not turn a dial yet.

Our first flight took us all around Oklahoma City and downtown. It was a beautiful clear day, and I thought we could see Texas, but I'm not sure that was even possible. We landed back at Guthrie, and I helped Matt push the plane back into the hangar he was renting. Was I doing this? Pushing *our* plane into a hangar? Times have changed.

Matt continued to take flight lessons and babysit open houses on weekends, and by now, he was getting more proficient with his myoelectric arm. We were learning that a prosthesis is an amazing device, but certainly not quite as good as your own arm and hand. It had some quirks, and there was no way Matt would have been able to pick up a coin with his fingers. According to everything we read, that was a bit down the road.

In the middle of June of that year, Matt and I got into the Trinidad and flew to Tulsa. He had an appointment with a DPE, Designate Pilot Examiner contractor, of the FAA. She would conduct a flight with Matt for him to regain his instructor licenses. They were gone for about a half hour. When they came in, they both looked exhausted. It was just so hot.

She said to me, "Solid pass with flying colors!" She added, "Your son is an amazing pilot. You can fly anywhere with him!"

Such sweet words to hear. We flew home in the heat, pushed the plane into the hangar—I was getting good at this—and headed for home. When we returned home, I told Matt I would start preparing dinner, and he said he had an errand to run. I wondered to myself, *What's he up to?* I found out about an hour later when Matt returned home. He was carrying a dark green material over his arm, and it looked like there were hangers attached to the material. Yes, dark green shirts advertising a flight school at the airport. Matt had landed a job as a flight instructor and would be starting work the next morning!

Matt had no students, obviously, but he put on his uniform and shirt, and he was off to work before 7:00 a.m. My gosh, how we had advanced! He would stay at the flight school all day, break for a Subway sandwich, hang around in the afternoon, and come home at dinnertime.

When we questioned Matt about his day, he said he watched planes coming and going, he talked to pilots coming into the FBO (flight based operation), heard all about the goings-on at other private airports, and studied all the air charts in the event he had a flight. He wanted to make sure he knew where he was going.

On the third or fourth day, Matt came home and announced, "I have a student!" He did, indeed. Turned out his student was a man named Dr. Kent Smith, and he was the president of Langston University. Kent liked early morning lessons so he could go straight to work after flying. Matt, despite not being a morning person, never complained about having to be at the airport for a 7:00 a.m. flight. He sure did love what he was doing.

At the end of the week, he told us he had to go back to the airport after sundown to do six touch-and-go landings to be current at night time. Off we went to the airport with Matt. He and Jeremy pulled the Trinidad out of the hangar. He climbed in and taxied to the runway. Jeremy was holding a transceiver so we would hear Matt's radio calls. We watched in the dark as he lifted off. Jeremy and I stood there on the tarmac and cried. I don't know if Matt knew we were so emotional, and I'm pretty sure we didn't tell him.

On his sixth and final landing, we pulled ourselves together and started walking to the hangar. Matt pulled up behind us, cut the engine, and jumped out of the plane. "Did you see those landings, folks? All greasers!" Which meant he was pleased with the landings. Matt and his dad discussed landings and speed on our way home, and they continued their discussion late into the night.

The next morning Matt was up real early, and he was on his way to work. He would be meeting his second student for a flight.

I congratulated Matt on acquiring another student and wished him a good day. I certainly never told him that I would not use the phrase, "Blue Skies and Tail Winds." I guess I had become somewhat superstitious. I learned later in the morning that the mysterious second student was Jeremy! My two guys were so excited to be doing this. Matt left early so he could get the Piper Cherokee ready with a pre-flighting before his lesson took place.

Matt continued to accrue new students and seemed to love what he was doing. He particularly loved check ride day. He would leave the house early in the morning and give flight lessons until the student taking the check ride would arrive. Then it would be time for some ground school review and possibly a short review flight. There are photos of all the students who have passed the check ride. They all stand in front of the plane with Matt and the FAA agent proudly holding their private pilot's license. Jeremy got his license on his birthday on a cold, sun-filled day in January. I love the photo.

Matt continued his job at this flight school for a couple more years, and there were lots of private pilot licenses earned. Needless to say, Jeremy and I were so proud of Matt and all his accomplishments. I so wished I could speak with one of the nurses from the burn ICU and tell her, "You were right!" After everyone on the burn team was sure Matt would survive, she had said to me, "He will fly around again!

I had said to her, "Are you nuts?"

She had laughed and said I would be back in a few years to tell her what Matt was doing and what he was flying. She was the mom of three or four boys, I believe, and she'd insisted she was right.

We all continued to heal and do well. I really believe that by supporting each other, we were creating a new life for ourselves. Life had changed, but in many ways it was still the same. Matt continued going to the airport and flying with all his students. At one point he had about 10–12 students, which kept him extremely busy.

He said to me one day, "Hey, Ma, I have an idea! I'll run it by you at dinner when Dad gets home!"

All of Matt's ideas seemed to focus around flying and airplanes, so I was anxious to hear what he was planning!

CHAPTER
SEVENTEEN

Matt's new idea was a doozy! After dinner he said to his dad and me, "I think I'll start my own flight school!" We were flabbergasted and had lots of questions like "where, when, how?" He told us to sit down and he would tell us all. There was a huge empty hangar on the other side of the airport. If he could purchase that, he could turn it into a school.

He got in touch with the owner, and after going back and forth with him, he agreed to sell the hangar to Matt. The hangar had been in his family for a long time and had been owned by his father and grandfather, I believe. He was very emotional about the sale, but he was very excited about another flight school coming to the airport. We probably had hundreds of hours of discussions with Matt about his newest endeavour. We went over numbers. Can he afford to do this? Does he know how to do this? Does he need to hire help? And if so, where will he find the help?

Matt decided to get in touch with an old friend and instructor from Flight Safety. He was no longer at the school in Vero Beach, Florida, but living with his family in Northern California. Matt offered him a job as a flight instructor and assistant to Matt. He was hoping his friend could help him get the school going.

Next on the list after the purchase of the hangar was finding a couple of planes. Matt did a lot of research and decided one of the best training planes is the Cessna 172M. He went somewhere in the Nebraska, where he got his first Cessna, a 1973 172m model in white with beautiful blue stripes. Matt lovingly called his first plane "Ole Blue."

Some renovation was being done at the hangar, too. Matt added a classroom and a bathroom and, of course, painted and did a major cleanup. He decided to call his school Blue Skies Flight School. It would open on April 13, 2015.

Matt's friend from Northern California showed up at our house on a Sunday afternoon driving a rickety U-Haul with all his worldly possessions. He and Matt took all his belongings to the hangar. We learned that all his licenses had lapsed, so we weren't sure what he had been doing in the almost ten years since the guys had seen each other. He would have to do what Matt did and take lessons with an instructor and pass a SODA ride with an FAA agent.

On some nights his friend would stay at the hangar and make aluminium "things." He made us a three-dimensional star of David called a merkaba, which is hanging on a branch from a tree in our backyard. I don't know if he was planning to sell his merkabas or keep them, but that seemed to be his main interest. When Matt suggested they take the Cessna up, he reluctantly agreed.

Matt told us that he flew the plane alone, and when he asked his friend to take over, he replied, "That's okay, you do it!" Matt was extremely disappointed that there was no interest flying and instructing, which was the reason for bringing him out to join Blue Skies.

On a beautiful Sunday in mid-April, we celebrated the grand opening of Blue Skies Flight School. We ran a ribbon across the open hangar door. We invited our friends and rented folding chairs. Our rabbi came and offered Matt congratulations and talked about Matt's hard work, his perseverance and tenacity, and, most of all, his integrity. That is one of my favorite words ever and I was so proud that Rabbi would use that word to describe Matt.

Someone had given Matt a barbeque, and a friend of ours was grilling hamburgers and hot dogs. Three hundred people showed up! We did not have enough chairs, and we needed to replenish the supply of food a few times. Channel 4 showed up once again and filmed our rabbi speaking, and they had a shot of the audience applauding, and they even got a great shot of Matt cutting the ribbon. The reporter asked to interview Jeremy and me, but we declined. This was Matt's day, and it needed to be all about him. We watched the five o'clock news, and there it was, the clips about Blue Skies. They even showed the school's phone number on the screen in case anyone wanted to learn to fly in OKC. We think Matt did receive a few inquiries about lessons.

We discussed with Matt what he should do about his friend, since it was obvious there was no interest whatsoever in earning lapsed licenses or getting the school going. It looked to us like he wanted a place to sleep and a table for him to make his aluminium extrusions. When the airport manager came to Matt and said, "Is your friend sleeping at the hangar? Someone had observed him in pajamas near the wind sock." The manager continued, "We just can't allow that!" Matt was so disappointed, but he knew it was time for his friend to move out of our house and start living on his own. He told us his sister was sending him money so he could buy a car. Matt helped him find an affordable car, and he moved out of our house and found a trailer to live in somewhere in town. I had to use Clorox and Lysol in our guest room, and I wondered how people could be so disrespectful in someone else's house. That wasn't the issue, though. Matt would be at the school at 7:00 a.m. and would start flying early. The phone was ringing, people were showing up in his office, and the only peace he got during the day was when he was up in the air. I offered to answer the phones for him or go into the office to greet people, but he said he could handle it. I certainly understood. Matt was now a very busy business owner, and he certainly did not want his mom around. Life was really turning out to be beautiful!

We had lots of fun going to airport days with Matt. We loved watching his planes take off and land as he took airport visitors for free rides. We loved meeting his students, and we certainly loved all the positive feedback we got from the students about how conscientious Matt was and what a nut he has about safety, maintenance, and weather. As one student once told us, he was so comfortable flying with Matt, who, he felt, knew all about what *not* to do in the plane. We have heard that comment over and over these last few years.

Parents never get tired of hearing good things about their kids.

CHAPTER
EIGHTEEN

We had settled into a really great life. We had survived a tough situation in our family, and we never gave up. Matt was doing some socializing with fellow pilots and some students that were his age. Jeremy and I were always thrilled when he was going out with his cronies because he needed friends. He was also dating a young gal named Angie. This was a big event in our house because after Tricia left, he had no dates. He might have had one or two here and there, but nothing significant. He seemed to really be interested in Angie.

I think it was July of 2017 when Matt came to his dad and me and told us that he and Angie were planning to get engaged. If this is what Matt wanted and it made him happy, then that made us happy and content, also.

Matt continued to work at the school. In fact, business was booming. So many good things were happening for Matt, and we couldn't be more pleased for him. A diamond ring was purchased, and Matt told us he planned to give it to Angie soon. This time, we were not invited to the dinner.

The doctors at Shands Hospital had told us it would take Matt years to recover, but we had no idea what that meant, and I had trouble understanding. Matt had certainly grown up a lot in the past ten to fifteen years and was making all his decisions and calling all the shots. Jeremy and I talked about how comforting that was for us. We were now experiencing what other parents had experienced, albeit a little bit later.

We watched Matt go from the hospital with a completely battered body to a completely self-sufficient guy with lots of self-confidence.

But there is more…

CHAPTER
NINETEEN

We woke up on March 20, 2018, the first day of spring. It was cold and breezy, but there was lots of sunshine. It was also Matt and Angie's wedding day. There would be no hoopla today, just a very low-key ceremony.

We picked up the bouquet for Angie and boutonniere for Matt and then we drove to a small chapel in downtown Oklahoma City. After the ceremony, we went to a very nice avant-garde restaurant for dinner.

The kids left for a bed-and-breakfast in southern Oklahoma and would spend a few days relaxing on their honeymoon before coming home and going back to work.

Getting into bed that night, a thought struck me: all my children were married and settled down, Jeremy and I now had five grandsons, everyone was doing what made them happy, and Jeremy and I were empty nesters. That was a beautiful word. And we vowed to enjoy it! It was our turn!

EPILOGUE

"Quitting is not an option!" I said as Matt asked me, "What will I do with my life? I'm a mess!"

I said, "Your body took a horrible beating, but you have a good brain. It's up to you to figure out a way to use it!" I said these words to Matt so many times that even I started to believe them.

Healing happened slowly. When the doctors told Jeremy and me it would take years for Matt to recover, I had no idea what they meant. Now I get it. Every step was an effort, first in the hospital and then at home. I watched Matt learn how to walk again at rehab and cried with him as he sat down on the makeshift stairs they had because he was too exhausted to go on. My heart broke when he said, "I was able to run up a flight of stairs at home and now I'm getting tired after climbing three!" I just told Matt how wonderfully he was recovering and we would take one day at a time.

Truthfully, I wanted my son back, but I felt like I was losing bits and pieces of him. Whenever things got really tough, what I observed about the two of us was, we worked harder. I pushed Matt to walk a bit more, and I made him do more mouth exercise. I didn't know that either of us had such drive and moxie. And I was beginning to learn a lot more about my son. He wanted his life back, and even though he knew things would never go back to the way they were before his accident, he was determined to create something that would work for him. He wanted to drive and see his friends and have a job and maybe find a nice girl and settle down, but how long would that take?

"Who will love me?" Matt asked. "I don't look like I did before."

I said, "The young lady that comes into your life will be very special. She will have a good heart. She will be kind, and she will recognize how special you are. She will see past only one arm, no ears, and scarred body!"

With that said, we both sat and cried for a bit. Matt said, "You're not at all objective because I'm your son!"

I said, "That's partially true, but I've always been able to recognize a good and decent person when they are right in from of me."

I was learning a lot about myself as I walked this journey with Matt. Life is certainly not a bowl of cherries, nice and sweet and covered with whipped cream. Sometimes it stinks and then what do you do? I learned that despite my ADD, I never stopped. I kept going, and by gosh, I took Matt with me. Now it was no means one-sided. He was there for me, too, and he would talk to me and sometimes comfort me, and despite his small stature, he has extremely strong shoulders that I used often. We are a great team. We are each other's greatest cheerleaders!

I find that I cry less these days, and I am no longer the emotional wimp that I was for a lot of years. Jeremy and I are thoroughly enjoying our life in our house with our two dogs. We love doing things together, even if it's just going to the grocery store.

Every now and then, I'm reminded of what we experienced. I can close my eyes, and every sight, every sound, ever smell of the burn ICU comes racing back. Dreaming about the ICU keeps me humble. I'm reminded of all the other people I met who were in the same position as I was: the young mom whose two-year-old pulled a pot of bubbling spaghetti sauce off the stove onto his head—I can't remember her name, but I certainly remember her tear-stained face—or the mom whose son put a fire cracker in a

PVC pipe, and when it didn't go off, he looked in the pipe to see what was the delay. Of course, that's when it exploded, burning his face, or what was left of it and taking off his hand, which was holding the pipe. Accidents all of them, but life changing for every one of us. There were so many patients that passed through the unit, and so many that left the unit quickly on their way to the morgue, I presume. I had told Jeremy there was no way in hell I could let Matt be wheeled out of his room with a sheet over his body. So I prayed a lot. And I was grateful for every day that I was buzzed into the unit. That meant Matt was still there.

Someone told me a couple of years ago that Matt's ship has already sailed. This person said, "No one gives a shit about Matt and his accident. No one cares that he lost an arm, so get over it!" The hurt was pretty awful, because that ship that supposedly sailed is parked in our driveway. Jeremy and I will never get over almost losing our son, but as I said, we learned a number of harsh lessons. There is a handful of "friends" that I've not heard from since that fateful day. I'm sure they just didn't know what to say to Jeremy and me. I guess they also were not "friends."

Despite the awfulness of the accident and the severity of Matt's injuries, he and I have discussed who we have become. We both like ourselves. We like the strength we have acquired, and somewhere down the recovery road, we both become more patient and tolerant.

We hope that nothing like this ever happens in your family, but if it does, know that you will get through it. Lean on each other because that's what families do. Cry together, curse together, get angry together, but don't ever give up. Most importantly, don't forget to tell each other how much you love each other. Take one day at a time and you will heal!

ACKNOWLEDGMENTS

Someone told me a while back that I should write a book. I should write about my experience in a burn unit and let everyone know what I learned, what I felt, what I wanted others to know. I decided that might be a good idea.

When I started writing, I had no idea it was such a big deal and lengthy process. I was in for a surprise. My heart is in this book. Every word I wrote is exactly as it happened. I used names only if I was given permission to use them; for others, I just used first names.

First of all, I'd like to thank the most important man to ever cross paths with us: Dr. David Mozingo at Shands Hospital in Gainesville, Florida. In case I forgot, thank you for our son. Thank you for taking such good care of Matt and explaining everything to me so I could understand what was happening. Your expertise, knowledge, and brilliance are greatly appreciated.

A hearty shout-out to our dear friend Yard Dog, a.k.a. Jason Williams, a nurse in the unit. Whenever I saw him walk into Matt's room at the 3:00 p.m. shift change, I knew I could relax and maybe even run out for a sandwich because I knew Matt was in good hands. All the nurses were wonderful, but somehow we were becoming family with Big Yard Dog. Whenever we fly to Florida, which is usually to pick up our plane at the avionics shop, we always spend time with Big Yard Dog and his beautiful family. Thanks for all the hugs and words of encouragement, and a special thanks for teaching me how to do wound care on Matt's legs. We did that religiously for almost two years!

And then there is Bruce Butler, who always made me smile. You were the first one to make me believe in myself and assure me that I was in control. I can still feel your hands on my shoulders as you pushed me out of Matt's room when his ear fell into my hand. You were so calm and took such good care of me. You and Thais have become extended family also. Your wedding was an event we remember fondly.

Many thanks to Sue Mary and Jody, who were the ladies in the unit that I spent a lot of time with listening to and learning from. They were very wise, and I was in awe of them. They knew so much. I don't know why we didn't keep in touch, but I remember them with great fondness.

Dr. Peter Grossman, a great physician and artist. Thank you for doing all those surgeries on Matt's lips, mouth, and eyelids. Matt recently said, "Dr. Grossman put my face back together!" Jeremy and I agreed. We were so fortunate to have you so close to us in Los Angeles. Thank you for all your help.

Thank you to my publishing team for helping me get this project off the ground! What fun this has been!

Jeremy, my love, my best friend, my guy, this was tough on us, wasn't it? There were times when I though there was nothing left for us, but quitting is not an option! You and I have lived through a very unique situation, and we are both strong and tenacious people. And we have a great love for each other. Thank you for putting up with me, thank you for laughing at my jokes, thank you for taking me on romantic dates to the grocery store, and thank you for being mine! Thank you for reading my manuscript and being so supportive. I love you!

And a hearty thank-you for my daughter-in-law, Angie. You indeed were the gal that came into Matt's life and with a kind heart and special love, overlooked his disabilities. Thank you for loving him and taking such good care of him. You are an amazing young lady, and I love you dearly.

—Gerry Cole

Young Matt
in 4th Grade
(1986)

Matt
High School Graduation
(1995)

Our Little Friend
Talahasee

Matt and Gerry
Visiting Dr. Mozingo
(2013)

Matt with his Father Jeremy Flying
(2020)

Wedding Day of Matt and Angie
March 20th 2018

Matt, Gerry, and Jeremy
on a Cruise last 2016

Attending a Friends wedding
and Matt was the best man
(2015)

Gerry and Jeremy
on a Cruise
(2017)

Thank you so much for reading our story.
Always remember **QUITTING IS NEVER AN OPTION**.

- The Cole's -

P.S. what part of our story struck you most?
Leave us a comment on where you got the book.

CPSIA information can be obtained
at www.ICGtesting.com
Printed in the USA
BVHW021051200921
617100BV00013B/291